RANDOM HOUSE

HOUSE

LARGE PRINT

Say Say Say

Say Say Say

Lila Savage

RANDOM HOUSE
LARGE PRINT

Copyright © 2019 by Lila Savage

All rights reserved.
Published in the United States of America by Random
House Large Print in association with
Alfred A. Knopf, an imprint of Penguin
Random House LLC, New York.

Cover art and design by Jenny Carrow

The Library of Congress has established a Cataloging-
in-Publication record for this title.

ISBN: 978-0-593-16458-7

www.penguinrandomhouse.com/large-print-format-books

FIRST LARGE PRINT EDITION

Printed in the United States of America

10 9 8 7 6 5 4 3 2 1

This Large Print edition published in accord with the
standards of the N.A.V.H.

for Essy
in memory of G.

Say Say Say

• I •

Later, looking back, Ella would be hard pressed to remember any details that had set this interview apart. It was sad, but then it was always sad, or Ella wouldn't be needed. She had been working as a companion for elderly people for six years, and somewhere along the way, sadness had lost its power to shock Ella the way it once had. It still reached her, but it was like recognizing a flavor, like eating a jelly bean without looking first to see what color it was. **Oh this,** she might think, **I know this taste. This is incremental loss. This is trying to remember. This is regret. This is forgetting, forgotten, gone. This flavor is grief.**

Jill was different from most of Ella's

other clients: she was young, only sixty, the victim of an accident rather than the mental and physical crush of age. The tragedy of such premature loss was unfamiliar to Ella, but she stepped up to it dutifully, felt for its contours, pressed the tip of her tongue to its bitterness, and, ultimately, shouldered its weight. What was her burden compared to Jill's? Compared to those who loved her?

She had liked them, immediately and more than usual. She felt they might have been friends, **ordinary** friends, were the circumstances ordinary, which, of course, they weren't. Nick, Jill's son, was only a few years older than Ella, and he had an endearing sincerity to him, not earnestness but an unusual frankness, as though he couldn't be bothered to dilute his humor or irritation or sadness into the tepid, circumspect conversation of most people. His father, Bryn, had an easy charm about him, and only his increasing talkativeness as he warmed up to Ella betrayed how isolating his circumstances must be. They had been dealing with the aftermath of Jill's car accident and head injury for more than a decade now. Jill had seemed mostly herself for a while, but then came the crying, and the tantrums that seemed out of all proportion, and now she was sometimes like an advanced Alzheimer's patient, mumbling semi-coherently, wandering around, requiring near-constant supervision. Bryn had retired three years earlier to care for her, and her needs had only grown since then. Nick helped as much as he could, usually on weekends, but he and his wife lived up in Hinckley and couldn't realistically drive into Minneapolis more than once a week.

They had gathered in the living room for the interview, with Ella a lonely figure on the puffy leather couch and the two men standing, as though resting might betray how weary they truly were.

"I hope this doesn't sound creepy," Nick said, "but once I learned your full name I checked to see if we have any Facebook friends in common. You know Trent Olson?" She nodded and he smiled with real friendliness, although there was a restlessness to his bearing that had probably read as hyperactivity when he was a child and, now that he was in his thirties, looked more like athleticism, maybe. But though his was the kind of masculinity that held little appeal for Ella, she watched for cues he might be flirting with her.

Nick excused himself to go check on Jill, leaving Bryn and Ella to themselves. Bryn seemed pleased that he would have more time to explore interests outside of caregiving, and also pleased that he had someone to discuss it with.

"We're too deep into spring to do everything I want in the garden," Bryn said, "but soon there will be tons of green beans to pick, and raspberries, and zucchini, and then we'll really get into tomato season. Jill used to be able to help with the harvesting but not anymore. I could occupy her for nearly an hour at a time picking raspberries on a nice day, until eventually she began to see it as a chore, and then she could no longer do it anyway." He relayed these stages of decline with what seemed an easy candor.

"Do you grow any rhubarb?" Ella asked.

"Not really on purpose, but there's some that keeps stubbornly coming up on the side of the house."

"I like to make chilled sweet rhubarb soup, it's so summery. But I live in an apartment now so I can't grow my own and it seems wrong to buy rhubarb in a grocery store."

"I know what you mean. When Nick was small, he would take a juice glass of sugar out to the rhubarb patch and break stems off to dip and eat. It's not a grocery-store kind of food."

Again Ella checked to see how this nostalgia registered on Bryn's face and found that his eyes were smiling with an uncomplicated cheerfulness that matched his grin.

"I'd like to sign up for a Community Ed class or two also," Bryn said. "Since I retired to take care of Jill, I haven't kept pace with the latest technology for carpentry."

As he described the dimensional capabilities of computer programs for woodworking, Ella decided they **would** become friends. A more sentimental or less experienced caregiver might have assumed that this didn't require deciding, but Ella had done some version of this many times with others, and had learned early on the benefits of some degree of detachment. Ella usually found clients through her Craigslist ad, and sometimes through word of mouth, because an agency would take too large a cut and would require her to have a car. Her first client had been her friend Jake's grandmother, whom she had known and cared about before the fog descended; Ella had been job hunting after dropping out of graduate school when Jake's mom had asked, "Could you visit my mother a few days a week?" At first Ella had been shocked that she could earn even a meager living this way (fifteen dollars an hour to start, twenty after the first year), just listening to Betty's meandering stories, making sandwiches, playing checkers, feeding the ducks. With Betty, Ella had remained wide open; as the weeks and months progressed, the air between the two women had become charged like metal or water conducting electricity, the pangs of loss and death intermittent but shocking. If Betty didn't answer the door of her senior apartment, Ella would feel panic swell in her throat; her body would prepare itself for impact as she scurried to find some staff member with a master key. Each time, Betty would have been napping, or getting her hair done in the basement of the building, or using the bathroom, and Ella would cry with relief, shaken and grateful, like the mother of a child who has stopped one step away from the path of a speeding bus. This was not a sustainable response, not for all the workdays in a week, all the weeks in a year, six years, half a dozen clients and counting.

And so Ella had learned to step in and out of grief, to sample it on demand. She didn't seek to block it out entirely because the poignancy was among the few rewards of the job. It was a strange way to make a living: the slow creep of hours, the tedium of domesticity and isolation, morning talk shows bleeding into drowsy afternoon soaps, all pierced with looming mortality and surreal delusions. She would succumb to the boredom and drift, as though submerged in a lake. The cool water would tug her gently; sounds were muffled, it was tranquil, and then something would compel her to burst through the surface and confront the frailty and sorrow and humiliation of decline. For a moment, she would be fully present in this sadness, porous in her empathy. It was almost unbearable, but at the same time, it seemed like a gift, to feel so much. She began to feel, rather than know, that the promise of death infused the adrenaline of living, and she was grateful to have this lesson at so little personal cost, because the tragedy belonged to someone who'd begun as a stranger.

Ella alternated between certainty that her true talents were wasted in this unskilled service work and another kind of certainty, that each action she took mattered, whether it was changing a soiled disposable brief with kindness and tact or listening to a tedious reminiscence for the thousandth time, so that someone whose self was slipping from them might clutch it for a moment longer. The truth contained both of these elements but was far more complicated. Ella had other talents, though perhaps none were greater than these; what were her elaborate meals or mediocre paintings to anyone but her? And if this caregiving, this tact and empathy, represented the best she had to offer, then it was also true that she offered these gifts as infrequently as she wrote her occasional poem. More often than not, she browsed through a magazine, she micro-waved a hot dog, she did laundry just for an excuse to leave the room, she drifted in her mental lake as her client dozed—it all hinged upon her whim. And then there was this other nagging concern: the way her role often felt uncomfortably voyeuristic—she could hold it all at arm's length, even if only for a while.

Nick came back into the room and said, with a laugh but also a degree of the derision grown sons are inclined to display toward their fathers, "Dad, stop boring Ella. I'm sure she has places to be." It wasn't that Bryn was being inappropriate; it was more like Nick saw the tang of his father's loneliness as a reflection on him. Although Bryn remained smiling, his voice took on an edge as he responded to Nick. "We're just getting acquainted," he said.

"Oh, before you go, would you like to meet my mom?" Nick asked, turning toward Ella in a way that seemed to subtly exclude Bryn.

"Of course," Ella said, making eye contact with Bryn as though it were his question she was answering. The three of them followed the sound of a television down a dim hallway and into a small den. Ella expected Jill to be sitting, but she stood with her back partially turned away from the television and a naked plastic baby doll in her hands. Jill looked so much younger than Ella expected that it startled her, momentarily, out of her detached professionalism. Jill was slim, and there was no gray in her curly red hair. Her freckled face was nearly unlined except for the deepening channels that ran from the sides of her nose to the corners of her mouth, and the reading glasses perched on her delicately pointed nose suggested that she had perhaps just set down an interesting magazine article to perform her role as hostess.

"Hello," Ella said. "So nice to meet you. What a pleasant room." She turned as though admiring it, took in the windows illuminated by afternoon sun and the old, dark-stained built-in bookshelf. Eventually she would come to have each title and trinket it contained memorized, but today she turned back to Jill to see how her greeting was being received. Jill seemed agitated, although it was difficult to tell if this was in response to the newly crowded room. She muttered something beneath her breath; Ella couldn't tell if it was addressed to her or to the doll. Bryn stepped closer to Jill and put an arm around her, squeezing her into a brief side hug. Ella observed that they seemed at once just like a long-married couple in that moment of casual affection and entirely unlike one in the clear disparity between their capacities.

"Say say say," Jill said, and then she crooned lovingly to the doll, ran a dirty-nailed finger down the doll's plump cheek.

· **2** ·

Ella boarded the bus to go see Sharon, and looked doubtfully at the sundress she'd worn for her interview. She had been pleased and relieved to be offered the position with Jill, but she knew that she still couldn't afford to give up her occasional work elsewhere, Alix's parents were still helping with the rent. She would start with Jill the following week, part-time at first but likely with increasing hours, which was generally how it went. Families' needs increased, and Ella became increasingly indispensable. She would keep her monthly shifts with Sharon as insurance because all caregiving work was inherently temp work:

the need for her assistance could end at any moment.

She hoped Sharon wouldn't have anything really dirty for her to do today, even though it was difficult to imagine what tidy tasks there might be. Perhaps baking more cookies. Ella actually thought that would be worse than ruining the sundress with toilet bowl cleaner, because Sharon was already so overweight that it prevented her from leaving her house for anything less than a doctor's appointment or a funeral. It put Ella in a tricky position—trickier, in a way, than usual—because these shifts with Sharon, picked up here and there while she looked for steadier hours, were at Sharon's impetus; Ella answered only to her, and not her adult children, as was so often the case. If Sharon wanted four dozen cookies, Ella couldn't say, "I'd love to, but your son says your doctor has forbidden it." There was no buffer, no absent authority to invoke. (Sharon's children visited, occasionally while Ella was there, but they spoke **at** their mother in agitated voices instead of **to** her, and they never sat down.) Ella would just set out the unsalted butter to soften and begin cracking eggs into the precise mixing bowl that Sharon directed her to in her singsong trills. Ella felt almost like a submissive hired by a fetishist, and, in a sense, she was, for Sharon knew the contents of every kitchen cabinet with the penetrating familiarity of a devotee, and her instructions for Ella, who was certainly capable of baking chocolate chip cookies, were exacting and almost tremulously eager.

It might seem cozy with the two women in the kitchen, chatting, Ella in the apron Sharon used to wear, breathing in the scent of vanilla extract and brown sugar, but Sharon could no longer fit into the apron, couldn't even fit into the largest disposable briefs, and so put incontinence pads on the few chairs she rotated among, leaving a new spot of urine each time she laboriously rose, and the smell of urine, to which her incontinent dog contributed, overpowered the more pleasant aroma emanating from the oven. Sharon never stopped talking.

She would sit in her soiled muumuu, her hair floating in fine tufts around her clearly visible scalp, and hold forth on four subjects in heavy rotation: her beloved dog, Argus; what, exactly, Ella should be doing at any given moment; her **foodies** (the things she wanted to eat, or have someone buy and deliver, or used to eat, or used to cook, or had a coupon for, or had found advertised in a grocery circular, now as creased and lovingly fondled as an old issue of **Penthouse**); and the Blessings of Our Heavenly Father, of Whom We Are Not Worthy, Lord Jesus, Lord Jesus, Gracious Heavenly Father, Blessed Be, Who Died for Our Sins, and We Are Not Worthy, Blessed Be.

The worst of it wasn't the smell of urine, or the hallelujah spoken word, or the scrubbing of the portable commode, or Ella's troubling complicity in Sharon's food addiction, or even the photo, hung in an out-of-the-way corner, of Sharon, scorchingly beautiful in a wedding dress, with a luxuriant mass of hair and an incredibly tiny waist. The worst of it was that Ella liked Sharon. Her eyes were kind and sad, and sometimes, when the hallelujahs would dwindle and then sputter, for a moment she would speak in the voice of a different woman, one who was smart, self-aware, and utterly defeated. In such moments, she didn't seem so different from Ella, who knew something of the shame of having a body that demanded more than it required, and also of the comforts of the Holy. Ella's sympathy for Sharon was almost distinct from her sympathy for Sharon's body, a despised mass Sharon was tethered to, unable to forgive for its betrayal, and Ella almost wanted to soothe it, like a wounded creature. It wasn't her **body's** fault that it was cumbersome, and chafed, and snaked with fleshy crevices that were difficult to keep clean, Ella would think, exhaling a puff of grace she never extended to her own physical form.

Ella wished she could somehow keep Sharon present with her in those quiet moments, those sad, lucid chinks in her chattering armor, though in the end, they were just moments. Ella didn't blame her, really, for wanting to drift out of her semi-squalid disappointment and into Jesus's arms or into the **Fearless Flyer**'s exquisite promise of tri-tip steak, but it was disheartening. Honey-sweetie-darling, Sharon would say to her, you're an angel, sugar, you're a lifesaver, dear girl, what would I ever do without you? The endearments were like veils; it almost felt like Sharon couldn't look directly at her, like she was talking around Ella's silhouette without seeing her, and the loneliness hung thick between them, evidence that Ella had failed at the only part of the job that mattered.

· 3 ·

Ella had met Alix at a party she went to with Cissy four years earlier. Cissy was older than Ella, and everyone at the parties she went to seemed like legitimate grown-ups, bearded men with eyes that crinkled at the corners when they smiled at Ella, and stylish, lipsticked women looking voluptuously dishier and fifteen pounds heavier than Ella imagined they had in their twenties. At that time in her life, the parties Ella more usually went to were either full of people she had graduated from college with or throngs of young, largely homogenous gay men, their eyebrows as unnaturally groomed as Jean Harlow's.

The party was in a warehouse converted

into artists' studios, and Cissy had informed Ella on the way there that the rent was crazy cheap, because it was so close to a Superfund site that people couldn't safely live there full-time. This had struck Ella as attractively dangerous and bohemian, but she had noted, as usual, that Cissy took an annoying amount of satisfaction in impressing her, in making her feel privileged to be included. Cissy's friend Isaac drove them there. He needed to get out of the house because he had become a bit reclusive in the few months since his wife had left him, and the prospect of this divorce only served to make Ella feel even younger.

They wandered around the warehouse, looking at strange, messy, occasionally gorgeous installation pieces and striking, slightly drunk artists. The space was so enormous that there might have been a hundred people present without it feeling like a crowd; they milled about a pile of mannequin parts twenty feet high and a claw-footed bathtub filled with moss and ferns and sat on old beauty salon chairs and battered plaid couches. Cissy knew lots of people there and fell into conversation easily, but Ella hung back a little. Isaac, perhaps chivalrously, stayed with Ella, and she was grateful.

Partially through their second drinks they found themselves sprawled on a fifteen-foot sectional, still roomily half empty, with a handful of people dispersed around it. Ella lazily noted that her bare knee and Isaac's were touching and assumed it was deliberate on his part. Isaac was appealing enough but not exactly her type; still, she enjoyed the attention, so long as it didn't carry the weight of further expectations. They hadn't been talking much before, although the music wasn't so loud that they couldn't, but they now seemed at ease with one another, exchanging carelessly knowing glances and the occasional witty, forgettable observation. Cissy had disappeared. A group of three meandered over and settled near them on the couch, and Ella observed them as though she were actually at a discreet distance. There was a girl with long dreadlocks and a tall man with scruffy facial hair, and the two of them were arguing with an irritable familiarity.

Closest to Ella was a very pretty girl, approximately her age, with enormous brown eyes and a dancer's legs. She was wearing a frilly vintage dress covered in lace that must have looked fussy on its hanger at Goodwill but on her looked frothily chic. Her expression was both anxious and bored, and she seemed content to be excluded from her friends' disagreement.

"Hello," she said, shifting slightly to look at Ella, who was normally shy under such circumstances yet felt somehow liberated by the languid persona she had adopted with Isaac.

"I like your dress," Ella replied. The girl cringed a little and looked down at the scalloped hem as though she had been hoping Ella wouldn't notice. "Oh. No . . . ," the girl said, and then: "As soon as I saw you in that dress, with that necklace, I wanted to meet you."

"Thank you," Ella said, with a look

that hovered between humility and self-satisfaction. Ella seldom had trouble receiving a compliment, mostly due to the alchemy of her good looks combining with the defiant bravado of being more plump than was fashionable.

Ella managed to tease out of the girl that she was a barista and also a printmaker and painter, that she was dating the tall, scruffy man, and that her name was Alix. Unlike virtually everyone else at the party, Alix made Ella feel older. She was wide-eyed in her self-deprecation, and her eagerness to become friends seemed exaggerated for effect, like performing a child's playground overture. Gradually, Ella forgot to keep her knee against Isaac's, and then forgot to include him at all. The impression of a playground overture proved astute; it felt like one of those chance encounters from childhood that soon turned into a cheerful, furious argument about who is the captain and who is the skipper of their imaginary ship. But Ella knew that this kind of imme-diate intimacy could often be just as easily forgotten, and so she wrote her phone number on Alix's hand before she left.

Once Alix was gone, Ella leaned apologetically into the shoulder of poor, neglected Isaac, a posture that left her still feeling rather like a girl, now worn out from play, except Ella wasn't tired. She liked the feel of Isaac's worn T-shirt against her cheek, and the warm, masculine smell of him. He agreeably slipped his arm around her shoulders. If this gesture had struck Ella as sexually assertive, she would likely have eased apart, but it seemed companionable, and it occurred to her that maybe he was sad about his divorce in a way that tamed his appetites. Soon enough, though, they were back into their earlier groove of intermittent banter with a low hum of attraction. The space had become more crowded, and noisier, and so as not to feel removed from the reckless undercurrent that emerges as a party builds momentum, Ella dangled her legs across one of Isaac's knees as the sectional filled in around them. She still felt pleasantly languid and enjoyed the largely unfamiliar power of being uninvested in his interest. She admired the look of her own supple legs and her feet in the pretty high heels against Isaac's cut-off work pants. He rested a masculine hand just below her knee, and she saw that it wasn't a boy's hand, pink-palmed, sweatily self-conscious, but a man's hand, callused, one that worked at a trade—Isaac was an electrician—and that had, until recently, worn a wedding band. He stroked her leg lightly, almost absent-mindedly, as he chatted just loud enough to be heard. Ella's indifference dissolved into the first stirrings of desire. She still wasn't really attracted to Isaac—she thought, not quite accurately—just to his attraction to her. Somehow, Ella realized, he had played his cards in the only order that could have found him any degree of success: a little more deliberate and she would have shied away, a little bit less attentive and she would have begun to look around for someone else to give her attention.

After they dropped Cissy off, Ella permitted Isaac to kiss her in his truck outside her apartment. She kissed him matter-of-factly, as though it were fair for him to expect this much but no more. His tongue moved around her mouth with a pleasant confidence that didn't make demands, but Ella thought only about how soon she could politely disentangle herself and go inside. Her panties retained the memory of his coarse fingers on her leg at the party, but it was as if a boat lock had come down in her middle, and nothing that happened above the waist had any effect below it. She was closed, she had made herself unreachable, and she bid him a polite good night as she shut the truck's door and turned away, already checking to see if Alix had sent her a text.

Ella had a terrific apartment; the first time Alix came over, she was blown away by the space and by what Ella had done with it. It could have been the set of a certain type of movie, it was so carefully put together with thrifted and cast-off items. If Ella had doubts about her other creative outlets, she had none about this, about her capacities with the domestic arts; it was the one realm in which she felt no conflict between her lower-middle-class background and her potential departure from it. She hated the ugliness of the house she grew up in and found an almost mystical satisfaction in the hunting down of lovely objects at yard sales. Her income was far less than she might have wanted but it wasn't evident in looking around her home. A colorful, intricate wooden doll house sat on a battered coffee table that Ella had painted cerulean blue, and there were books and plants everywhere, and a swing suspended from the ceiling, and mismatched vintage pots hung all over the kitchen walls. One living room wall was entirely covered by a blown-up photograph of the countryside in the northwest of Russia. The trees were small and golden, and the sky had an eerie sublimated brightness. The photo had been printed out, glossy page by glossy page, and affixed in rows that formed a mural-sized whole. On the opposite wall were a series of prints Ella's aunt had made in the sixties, understated, abstract, in shades of black and navy. Nothing in the apartment looked new; everything had a patina of use. A wooden chair slung with caramel-colored leather looked design-significant but not necessarily weight-bearing; Ella had bought it at a yard sale. The sofa was long and low, its upholstery both faded and torn, but undeniably marvelous, with a pattern of aerial-view fields spreading like a green-and-gold patchwork quilt over its length.

This was where they had sat, that first visit, sipping cheap wine, becoming acquainted. The sun slipped below the horizon, leaving them illuminated only by the streetlight outside, with the noisy air conditioner turned off at this cooler hour of summer darkness. The windows that could be were open, and a humid nighttime breeze stirred the drapes and pulled strands of hair across their necks and cheeks. It was late, later than either of them had planned for, but the Thai food and then the art opening they had attended (good people-watching, disappointing art) had given them only a taste of all they might say to each other if they had the chance. Ella felt as if she had found a friendship that seemed so fated, so easy, so urgent that it was like falling in love, only more rare, and it was as if they had to tell each other everything, and as quickly as possible, interrupting an opinion with an anecdote, and interrupting that with the analysis of a movie, only to interrupt that with Important Plans.

Ella was describing her parents' divorce when Alix picked up her hand and examined the antique charm bracelet fastened around her wrist. This did not surprise Ella; it seemed in keeping with their casual intimacy, the way they had linked arms as they walked around the overchilled gallery space. But then Alix leaned in and kissed her, which surprised Ella. She had not anticipated this turn of events, but if she somehow had, she would have expected something quite different, something sweet, and girlish, and almost chaste, or implausibly posed and bloodless, like a photo shoot in **Vogue**. Instead, before she could think, Alix was straddling her, a knee clenched against each of Ella's hips, and they were kissing so deeply they were melting into each other, and then Alix was biting her, biting her lip, and then her cheek, leaving teeth marks against the flushed skin, and then her neck, and then Ella was doing the biting, it was Alix's breast, small and round in her mouth, and then they were stumbling to the bed.

They had both dated women before, interspersed with an assortment of men, but nothing had been quite like this. From the beginning, there were no predictable roles, no demure glances, no lingering touches, no laughing at jokes with an outsize hilarity. There was none of that, somehow it would have felt dishonest, it would have been at the expense of something else, some clarity or frankness, some unembarrassed sincerity they had pooled between them.

It happened fairly quickly, after that

first night. Two weeks of spending every possible moment together, and then Alix moved in. It had been convenient, meeting Alix just as Ella's previous roommate was leaving Minneapolis for law school in Chicago. They hadn't talked about whether it was a **forever** kind of relationship, they had just accepted that, for now, they wanted to ride whatever welcome crest this was. It was unbelievably heady to feel so profoundly **understood,** not like they were beyond words, but as though the words had a breathless inevitability about them, as if the depth of the other's interest was a psychic magnet, pulling their truest selves into articulation. It became Ella's favorite of nearly all activities, seeing herself as fascinating through the eyes of Alix. **Is this how men feel?** she wondered, suddenly, with a jolt of discomfort. Was this why they would ask women out to dinner and then never stop talking about themselves? A pretty girl as funhouse mirror, offering up ego-affirming distortions? The beauty of it was that she could talk about it with Alix, and, like nearly every subject, it became more interesting as they pulled it apart together.

Before they met, Ella and Alix had both preferred androgynous women, like painfully beautiful boys, with cowlicks and soft skin and square jaws and tattoos on the lean muscles of their biceps. They'd **kissed** feminine women, but who hadn't? In college? It came with the territory, but it had carried limited erotic weight. Now their similarities felt at once overwhelmingly sexy and gloriously deviant, like Lauren Bacall in her prime, throatily muttering "Fuck you" to all that was masculine in the world: the bearded radical Ella had dated at twenty-two who scoffed at her counter-revolutionary addiction to fashion magazines while insisting she continue to shave her legs. The musician Alix had been in love with who never once let her hang out with his male friends, as though her realm was the bedroom and his was the laddish larger world. The jock Ella had dated in college, who had made her stand, shivering, naked, while he jerked off, whimpering unsexily. The endless, unsought male attention Alix received in every bar, at every party, and, in contrast, for Ella, what she perceived as the nakedness of her **need** for sexual attention, on display for all to see in her lipsticked face and the pivot of her walk. Her unsubtlety felt inseparable from her femaleness, the abhorrent softness of her body, the lavishly pantomimed Eros that was the soldered flip side to her placating hesitancy, the infuriatingly routine feeling of supplication, of being coolly assessed and found wanting. It wasn't just the remarkable absence of all that, the sting of marginalization, of surging resentment inspired by the latest display of cheerful, boyish entitlement; it was the soaring relief of not having to explain it to one's beloved.

That evening, when Ella returned from her interview with Jill, Alix was there, stirring something difficult to identify on the stove and talking to her mother on the phone. It was lovely, in a way, having somebody cooking something warm to share when Ella was so tired, but Alix was a troublingly experimental cook, often combining ingredients because the colors looked good together (like curry powder in guacamole) or following the flawed logic that if something is good—butter, cream, sugar, cheese—more will be better. Ella liked being the better cook, and it came out in gleeful bursts of exasperation or, if an audience were gathered, dramatic retellings of Alix's more spectacular failures.

Eventually she and Alix sat across the kitchen table from each other, pushing the soft, pale broccoli around in the extraordinarily salty pesto and interrupting each other so consistently that not a single thought was completed by either of them:

"You want a **gun**? No you don't. You want to try on the idea—"

"Why not? Maybe I do want a gun. Maybe I want to protect our property if—"

"What **property**? My computer? Because people are lining up to—"

"Okay, so nobody wants **that,** but once they've broken in—"

"You would what? Shoot them? You wouldn't even wake—"

"But what if I did wake up? And didn't have a—"

"It's so tiring when you try to be provocative," Ella said, a little irritated. It **was** tiring, how Alix liked to try on ideas that clearly weren't good, the way another woman might flirt, in a dressing room, with a dress that didn't fit. Ella thought it was silly when the world was full of untested ideas, and dresses, that **might** fit. At the same time, this was part of what she liked about Alix, how she pulled Ella outside of her own compulsive efficiency. It wasn't that there was anything really useful in contemplating gun ownership, or even interesting, as far as Ella was concerned, but once one stopped questioning such positions, other interesting ideas were bound to slip by unexamined. There was a degree of unwelcome rigidity to Ella's thinking, born of efficiency, certainly, although also, one level deeper, of fear. It was like repurposing objects: Ella preferred to use things in the manner they were intended for—no weathered antique rakes used as tie racks or earrings sorted into egg cups for her. This was because she'd grown up buying everything secondhand, and it had been a constant concern, misusing something out of ignorance—like the time she had worn a vintage smock to high school, unaware that it was a maternity dress, or when she had tried carrying her schoolbooks in an unbleached canvas bag and a more affluent girl had commented, not unkindly, "Oh, that's the kind of bag we use when we shop at the co-op," and Ella had realized how incongruous this simple, wholesome object was in her life, picturing her father at Cub Foods, filling it with Cup O' Noodles and frozen potpies. Ella didn't want to be **wrong,** but she also didn't want to be unimaginative. It was difficult, trying to scramble for footing in the middle class while yearning to disdain bourgeois conventionality. Alix's willful absurdity was almost like a mild hallucinogen, swirling and refracting the map Ella was always squinting at discreetly, worriedly, like a self-conscious tourist who doesn't like where she's found herself but doesn't want to be identified as an outsider.

· 4 ·

At the interview, Ella had decided to err on the side of caution when she was introduced to Jill and to greet her as she might any person. It was Ella's default position, and it had never served her wrong, for what harm could there be in showing respect, even if the recipient remained unaware? And Jill had appeared cognizant that Ella was a new person, she'd seemed more or less aware that it was an introduction. Jill had seemed polite but wary in a way that was somehow different from a child; a child might have been bashful, mumbling with husky displeasure what adults expected to hear, whereas Jill's reluctance seemed authoritative.

"Yes," Jill had said, "here I am. Here I am. What? What?" Which almost made sense, but it was difficult to tell if that was by design or coincidental. Ella had made her voice smile but tried to keep her cheer from seeming patronizing, and so she hadn't simplified her language. It had seemed to Ella that Jill found her friendliness overfamiliar; Jill's caution came close to registering as dislike. This made Ella dislike herself a bit, looking at herself through Jill's eyes. It was Jill's weary sternness that read as the clearest evidence that she was a mature person enduring hardship, and Ella's disinclination to acknowledge those cues seemed somehow invalidating. But there would be ample opportunities to strike a better tone in the future.

Now, settling into a routine, it was still difficult to tell what Jill understood and what she didn't. This remained slippery to navigate until, eventually, each trail of clues led to the same emptiness, the same barren field. Only that was later, much later. At this time, there was still a painful, lingering uncertainty about Jill's depths, nourished by hints of awareness, like bread crumbs dropped from her restless hands.

While Ella had been hired as relief for Bryn, so that he might have time for things other than caring for Jill, it was several months before he was willing to leave the women alone in the house together. He didn't want Jill to feel abandoned; he was hoping that she would come to recognize Ella and feel comfortable with her. Ella's first shifts, therefore, were spent with both of them, like supervised visits, only not really, because Bryn was watching not to see how Ella would do, or even how Jill would do, but to ease them into acquaintance, like a matchmaker, or like a host at a party. He offered up little facts about Jill, with space to breathe around them, like "Jill was a social worker" or "Jill always liked to run in the morning," as though the silence between them was an oversight on Jill's part, like all they needed was the right jumping-off point, so that Ella could follow up with "Oh, my uncle's a social worker, what sort of social work do you do?" or "You must be very disciplined—I'm not much of a runner **or** a morning person." Of course, questions directed at Jill, if they were acknowledged at all, could be answered in only the most rudimentary fashion, and even that was only in Ella's early months, or maybe even only the early weeks.

One day when Bryn was preparing their tea, Ella tried, instead of neutral friendliness, a more wry tone, one that reflected the combination of sharpness and resignation Jill's posture suggested as she sat with one denim-clad leg casually crossing the other, wearing sunglasses that didn't appear to be hers, the arms trapping her hair against her temples instead of sliding under it. Ella said, unsmiling, "It's so hot out. I'm so sweaty." Jill didn't smile either, and Ella couldn't see her eyes behind the sunglasses. "Would you like to take off that jacket?" Ella asked, because Jill was wearing her usual fleece zip-up, and her bangs were damp with sweat. "No. No. I don't know. I don't know! Say say say," Jill responded, turning her head away from Ella and then standing to reach for the water glass that sat on the table. She slipped her fingers in purposefully, as though testing something, and then began to flick the water in small splashes over the cup's rim.

Jill couldn't really converse, not in any meaningful sense. She would repeat phrases over and over. One was "Everybody has their story. Everybody has their story. Everybody has their story." Sometimes Ella would respond, "What's your story, Jill?" and Jill would reply, "Me? I helped the women. I don't know. I don't know. I don't know. Everybody has their story." That was about the extent of any sort of exchange of ideas. As the next best thing, Ella began to respond to Jill's circular rants as though they were friends chatting, responding in a steady, sympathetic murmur, as though the natural back-and-forth of conversation were occurring.

"Of course I agree," Ella would say, "but

is that really the important part? I suppose we each have to decide for ourselves. And I really am fond of cookies made with molasses. But you know I never make them. Were you ever much into baking?"

"Say say!" Jill would respond. "The children. The children. And we have to come back. Yes. It's mine!"

"Of course it's yours," Ella would say. "It's your house. I'm only a guest, although I'm very glad to be here. And I noticed there's a bowl of strawberries from the garden on the buffet, I can smell them from here! The little ones are always the sweetest, don't you think? Red right up to the stem. I wonder how many berries you would need to make jam? That fly is so annoying—I wish you had a cat to kill it. Have you ever owned a cat, Jill?"

"It's mine. It's mine. And we go all the time. Say. Say. And the children! I helped the women. I don't know."

"I used to have a cat," Ella would say. "His name was Clarence and he was very fat and grumpy. He had big puffy fur and a big puffy tail and it was a lot of work to brush him. It was nice to brush him outside in the summer because the wind would just blow the discarded fur away, it would just tumble across the grass. I like your socks today, Jill, red is my favorite color. Do you have a favorite color?"

"It's mine. I don't know. I don't know. It's what we do."

"When Bryn comes back, we'll have some tea. I hope we have strawberries."

Eventually Bryn asked Ella if she really understood what Jill was saying, and Ella explained, a little embarrassed, that she didn't. She thought the pretense might make Jill feel less isolated, like she could still connect with other people, but it became clear that this wasn't so, especially in the weeks when she began to seem concerned that Ella was mocking her. She would become agitated and tearful, and any efforts to connect were regarded with suspicion bordering on fear. At that point Ella tried to give her a wide berth, interfering only if she started trashing the kitchen, or tried to leave the house, or clutched her crotch, suggesting she needed to use the bathroom.

Did Jill become more comfortable with Ella during those first few months? Yes—at least it seemed so, to some negligible degree, but really, these compensated klatches (the three of them always drank cheap, bitter tea from mismatched mugs, the tannin coating their tongues in chalky sheaths) served mostly to make Ella more comfortable with Jill. Paying her to spend time with both of them wasn't really necessary, Ella would think each time Bryn walked her to the door with a gentle thank-you and a few discreetly folded crisp twenties. She wasn't thirteen; she wouldn't panic if they were left alone together and Jill cried, or rattled the baby gate on its hinges, or didn't make it to the bathroom. If Ella and Jill didn't need to become acquainted, and did so only in the most superficial sense, the tea parties did serve another purpose, which was that Ella and Bryn became friends.

They would sit, triangulated around the sunny, bare dining room table, and if at first

Ella was formal, with both shoeless feet flat on the floor and her mug lightly gripped, mostly forgotten in one hand as she made polite inquiries and appropriate responses, it wasn't more than a week before her knees were tucked up to her chest, both hands wrapped around the mug's warmth, an easy laugh on her lips. This both surprised and did not surprise Ella; one is not a professional companion for long without a gift for easy camaraderie, or at least a skillful impression of such. She was accustomed to being interested in what she was told and also of being bored, and in either instance she gave the same impression of friendliness, sympathy, good humor, admiration— whatever the circumstances required. Once in a while Bryn would talk at length about something of only moderate interest to Ella, but she forgave him that because she never provided the usual cues of just-visible boredom or distinctly polite interest, the way she would with a friend who wasn't paying her to listen. However, there was, as Ella had predicted at the interview, a natural ease between them; they were both **agreeable** people, meaning mostly pleasant, mostly considerate, attentive, modest, kind, and this reduced some of the barriers—of age, of gender, of station, of the muttered sounds of loss seated between them.

Still, it was a strangely limited intimacy, it always was, no matter how much Ella loved a client, loved their family, because there was always a degree of withholding that came with being paid for her time. When Ella was working, she was like a therapist: she listened carefully; she cut short her own anecdotes when she sensed wandering interest. If any client had seemed genuinely more interested in listening than talking, Ella might have told them almost anything, for she was a naturally forthcoming person, but nobody ever was. Ella didn't blame them; she knew she would be the same in their position. Ella considered herself-as-listener the greatest unstated benefit to employing her. She drew people out with the skill of a reporter, the difference being that she wasn't trying to get any particular dirt. Instead, she was feeling her way toward the stories that most wanted to be told, and when people allowed themselves to sink into the telling, it was with pleasure, and relief, and almost a feeling of moral affirmation. Their lives, with Ella-as-listener, felt significant and sometimes even righteous, or so she told herself.

With some clients, Ella almost felt as though she were collecting their memories before they lost them; it was like the Dixie Chicks lyric about the woman with Alzheimer's: "I will carry it on / and let you forget." Over time, the stories would repeat, sometimes through hundreds of increasingly garbled retellings, and Ella would no longer seek to draw those clients out. They would have developed a taste for the telling that was almost a solitary pleasure, and Ella could daydream quietly, murmuring appropriate responses as if accompanying a familiar recording. Even if she hadn't liked Bryn (and she truly did) she would still have found it a relief to have a new conversation each time they met, and to have someone remember what she had said to them, so that it wasn't like speaking into a vacuum, sharing thoughts and feelings that could have been almost anything, so briefly were they grasped before swirling down the mental drain.

Ella's knowledge of Bryn grew daily, even though he told more about his life than about how it made him feel. She saw him look at Jill with a forced smile of real affection that whispered of grief. Like so many men of her father's generation—indeed, like so many men—he could better express anger and frustration than other emotions. Still, she learned, more and more, about his most profound losses, his fears, and also his deepest loves, and he knew nothing of hers. Bryn's view of her life was that it was like a trolley car, always heading around the same track. One day the trolley might pass a hot-dog vendor, or a woman with a poodle waiting to cross the street, or a car almost hitting a bicyclist. Although the weather could vary, the route never did.

What Ella had done over the weekend or an interesting bit of news she had heard on the radio, the latest thing she was reading or the new recipe she was hoping to try: these were the trivial bits of herself she offered up.

Ella assumed that she was merely following Bryn's lead in the surface pleasantries of these conversations, but there was evidence to the contrary. For instance, Ella made frequent mentions of "Alix and I," casual references to the structure of her outside life. One day she became confused as to whom Bryn was referring when saying **he**, and then it occurred to her that he meant Alix. She didn't correct him. It wasn't that she **wanted** him to believe she was partnered with a man, or that she had any reason to think it would make any sort of difference to him, it was just somehow peculiar, unpalatable, to broach the subject, "Excuse me, Alix is a **woman**, I'm queer, you see." It felt, in a way, too late, as though this could only have been addressed immediately or not at all, as if, at the time of their meeting, it might have been absorbed as easily as Ella's other, relatively inconsequential biographical details, but time had shifted the dynamic. It would now become a pronouncement or a confession, something unsettlingly private. She didn't generally share that part of her life with her clients, who were often—besides elderly—religious, conservative, and disinclined to examine their prejudices this late in the game. Never mind that Bryn matched only one of those descriptors: that of client.

· 5 ·

Nowadays, Ella would come, they would visit for a bit, and then Bryn would slip from the room for an hour or two, to putter around in the garden or the basement or the garage. At first Ella wasn't sure what to do when this happened; she'd never been in quite this position before, except when babysitting, on the rare occasions parents had things to get done around the house. It seemed wrong to simply sit in the same room with Jill, charging an hourly rate for her passivity, with Bryn so close at hand. She got some books from the library that listed activities for the memory-impaired. Almost all of them seemed beyond Jill, whose favorite hobbies included washing silverware without any soap and folding the same three towels over and over. One day Ella brought a muffin tin and a tub of antique buttons, with the idea that she could sort them together by color, but Jill just pushed them around carelessly before losing interest. Next, Ella asked Bryn for some family photos, hoping they would mean something to Jill, that they would spark recognition, a connection. Jill just picked through them as messily and blindly as she did a catalog or magazine, seeing them without really seeing them, but Ella examined each photo with an avidity that almost felt impolite.

The first photos Ella saw of Jill were post-accident, taken during an impaired but higher-functioning time. In them, Jill stood with Bryn and Nick, her gaze and smile somehow off, as though she were at a slight remove. She was a little plump in those pictures, and the weight looked wrong on her, like a thin person slightly bloated, clothes selected by someone uninvested, makeup only contributing to the dissonant picture.

Ella and Bryn sat side by side in the brilliant noon sun, every bit of the yard gilded by the light. There was no wind today and so the sun felt just on the cusp of too warm and the flush and shine of it on skin and hair seemed decadent. Jill stood a short distance away, facing them without noticing them, her nervous energy stilled for the moment without a discernible cause. Her hair looked a more vibrant shade of red than usual with the sun pouring over its asymmetrical mass, the left side squashed oddly to her head, as though she'd spent the entire night sleeping on it, the right springing in random snarls and tendrils just long enough to reach below her jaw. Ella felt she could see Jill's freckles multiply before her eyes, as though they would burst like sped-up buds captured by time-lapse photography. The speckles covered every bit of exposed skin. Jill's eyes were close to the color of both her freckles and her hair, a warm brown that just fell short of rust. If she'd had higher cheekbones her face would have looked more beautiful, more ethereal, despite her graying teeth and the anxious, unhappy tilt that confusion and distress gave all her features, but her cheeks hung hollow and a little loose below her eyes, and her mouth was a thin line. Her shoulders stooped in a way that hinted at masculine dejection, or perhaps in the absence of long-practiced feminine postures: Jill no longer carried herself with the burdensome knowledge of continual assessment womanhood so often brings. Her chest appeared flat under the loose chambray shirt, and her jeans hung from her narrow hips, sitting in permanent accordion creases behind her knees, and mismatched socks, one red, one gray, were visible under her maroon velour slippers.

Eventually Ella found pictures of young Jill, of a slender and pleasant-looking but not quite beautiful woman with wind in her long seventies-style hair, laughing, with willful eyes, and then a stark black-and-white photo of young Bryn shuffled to the top. He looked searingly, impossibly handsome, chiseled, fearless, with a mountain rising behind him, and Ella lingered with the photo in her hands as though she hoped to memorize it. It changed how she saw him, even though he was still good-looking. He was tall, his body was still lean and strong, his silver hair thick and shaggy. The sculpted bones of his face, once achingly beautiful, retained their graceful architecture under the more rugged skin of late middle age.

Bryn's most appealing feature, however, was his smile, and Ella now understood why: it was the smile of a beautiful person, a person accustomed to receiving one in return, for who could resist matching the smile of such an attractive man? He smiled easily, even facing these wrenching circumstances, and the warmth reached his eyes. It felt almost flirtatious without being sexual, it defaulted into a playful quality that

Ella found familiar because she navigated the world in a similar way, but there was a difference: Bryn charmed because it was habitual, because he could; Ella charmed because she wanted to be liked.

Bryn had carried the photos up from the basement, jumbled in a shoe box, and somehow the modesty of this vessel struck Ella as more heart-wrenching than any of the haunted images it contained. It seemed symbolic of their whole situation, or maybe, more specifically, of Bryn himself, of how he bore the burdens of remembering with a distinctly masculine lack of ostentation. For a moment his strength and his vulnerability seemed indistinguishable, and Ella recoiled, ever so slightly, from the abrupt intrusion of this knowledge. She couldn't **un**know it, and now the wince in his stride would always be visible, even in the periphery of her vision, even, perhaps, when her gaze was averted.

One day, with a sort of studied carelessness, Ella told Bryn, "You know that black-and-white photo of you with a mountain in the background? You were so handsome. You looked like a movie star." She had thought this would be like telling a grandfatherly figure that he had once been as dashing as Clark Gable, a throwaway compliment that Bryn might dismiss with gruff pleasure. It didn't feel like that at all, Ella realized too late, with heat creeping across her face. It had been weeks since she had held the photograph, but she **remembered** it so clearly. Bryn just grinned and said, "Thank you," as though it weren't a surprise, as though it were deserved but unsought, which it was.

· 6 ·

At last, Bryn was willing to leave Ella and Jill alone, and Ella felt that her probationary period was over and her real work was beginning. How difficult could it be? On that first day, Jill unlocked the front door and walked out into the sunshine. Ella managed to block the wooden gate that enclosed the yard before Jill got to the sidewalk, but what to do next? She tried to convince Jill that they should go back inside, only it was like trying to convince a cat of something; it was utterly wasted breath. She pleaded and reassured, she promised that Bryn would return to the house soon and expect to find them there; still Jill's hands remained clamped on the gate, ready to release herself should Ella step aside. Ella tried to lightly grip Jill's shoulder or hand, to guide her into the house, and Jill cringed away from her touch, yelling forcefully, and Ella feared that the neighbors would find something amiss. Likely this set of circumstances was just the sort of thing Bryn had feared might happen if he left them alone together too soon. They stood, almost immobilized in their standoff, for what felt like an hour, with Jill single-minded in her determination to escape.

Ella barely dared contemplate what might have happened if Jill had reached the gate first. Would Ella have been forced to chase her down and drag her inside? Was she strong enough to win a physical struggle? Would she have followed Jill down the city streets, interfering only if she tried to walk into traffic? How would Bryn have found them if that had happened? It was terrible to consider.

At last, Jill tried to make her way to the backyard, and Ella was able to corral her

toward the steps, since Jill moved predict-
ably away from her. When Ella finally closed
the front door behind them, she wanted
to blockade it with the sofa, but settled,
instead, for sitting on a wooden chair
directly in front of it, like a guard at her
station. It was unfortunate that Jill knew
how to unlock the door, that was true, but
as it turned out, only for another month or
two. Every skill was leaking from her.

Ella coaxed into being an idea of who
Jill was, who she had been; she sculpted
it inventively from the rough material she
was given. This was necessary, because Ella
felt the need to love Jill, and it was easier
to love a person. She tried to imagine the
life Jill and Bryn had shared before
the accident (seldom referenced, never
elaborated upon—Ella never heard
exactly what had happened) that had
changed their lives so abruptly. There was
something about the way Bryn carried himself that suggested Jill had taken the lead,
been the bold, perhaps slightly reckless one.
It seemed surprising, given that Bryn had

been the more physically beautiful of the two, though it also made a kind of sense. It wasn't that Bryn was weak-willed; he just seemed somehow to Ella like the younger brother to a decisive female, like he had something to prove, but also that he was accustomed to looking up to a more self-assured and perhaps exasperated woman.

Bryn spoke of his life with Jill, especially the early years, before Nick was born, as if it had been endlessly exciting: living abroad on the cheap, drifting through the seventies, picking up carpentry work here and there. He spoke of old friends from that time as though they still mattered to his self-conception, as if the value of his life was still somehow affirmed by these events and people and discussions and private jokes remembered across the decades. He sounded like he had prided himself on being an outsider, but an outsider who **belonged**. This belonging had something to do with those old friends, although it was most meaningfully rooted in the **we** of him and Jill; her fiery head next to his had turned the wandering into adventures, had rendered the lack of money bohemian, had made the creep of the years feel well spent.

Ella's life was yet short and uneventful, but still, she felt a distance between them that spoke more of temperament than age. She was not a **we** sort of person, despite her four years with Alix. Ella had never dreamed of being a **we,** she felt a distance between herself and other **we**'s, the girl who started every sentence with **my boyfriend** or **my girlfriend,** the people who followed their SOs around parties as if they would be lost without them. Even in this relationship, Ella thought of herself—and, when possible, referred to herself—in the singular. When she remembered road trips and parties and even the endless sociability of college, it wasn't the connections she had built with other people that seemed significant but the revelations about herself that the circumstances had enabled.

Bryn didn't just value belonging, he generously extended it to others. He was soon including Ella in the family's jokes and sayings, enveloping her in a friendly **we** that included himself, Jill, Nick, and Nick's wife, Lisa. He gave Ella crisp green beans from the garden, a bit of cherished sourdough starter, cuttings from houseplants she admired, first pick from the Goodwill donations. It didn't feel patronizing, although it might have, like a domestic worker wearing the castoffs of her wealthy mistress. Ella felt more like a daughter, like she rightfully should outrank the strangers picking through the thrift store shelves. Her table, where the silver-plated napkin rings ended up, felt like an extension of the family table. She pictured Bryn and Nick sifting through the buffet drawers, thinning the feminine detritus that Jill would never again polish and position on the Thanksgiving table. "Maybe Ella would want these," one might have said to the other, comforted, in a small way, by knowing where the unwanted objects might end up. But that was silly, Bryn was so unsentimental, he seemed to relish clearing the various surfaces of the long-occupied house. He was only being practical in his generosity.

Ella was accustomed to developing complicated relationships with the objects that belonged to her clients, especially those she worked long, regular hours with, over the course of months or years. Shopping for and cooking in two kitchens became confusing—was it Ella or Betty who was out of ketchup? For whom had she just bought a carton of eggs? And then she came to learn the exact shapes and locations of stains on the carpet, and every bit of Lladró or Belleek or Arabia in the china cabinet, the dusty dried flowers on the sideboard, the porcelain dish of gummy cough drops, the tattered wool runner tied to the high back of the rocking chair, the tea-bleed of rust on the bathtub enamel, like whiskers adorning the metal spout. Such familiarity became almost proprietary, as though seeing the objects every day gave her a kind of claim upon them, which wasn't to say that she **wanted** them, not usually, but rather, in the same way that a roommate might begin to feel like a sibling, as though the proximity translated into a knowledge tinged with belonging.

Sitting at her station, Ella looked around the living room and let the relief of boredom settle over her. Jill was folding towels again, making messy squares and shaking them out, smoothing, patting, matching corners badly. She hissed through her teeth as she worked, the sound interspersed with almost purposeful mumbling. Ella felt like an uninvited guest: What must Jill make of her presence? This strange girl sitting quietly in her house, watching her go about her business? Was Jill even aware of her when they weren't interacting? It was a peculiar kind of loneliness, sitting in that spare, bright room, almost silent but for the hissing, almost unoccupied but for the two of them. Ella looked at the potted lily; she thought about how there weren't any lamps in the room, or throw blankets, toss pillows, bookshelves, drapes. The gleaming coffee table was bare, floating on its muted area rug, a rectangle framed by a rectangle. Was this how Bryn had spent his days before he hired Ella? The minute hand moved incrementally; the sunbeams shifted to warm a new patch of floor. Was this how Ella would now spend hers? It was better than cleaning Sharon's portable commode, and yet a sadness seemed to infuse the sunbeam, seemed to reflect off the coffee table and the glossy leaves of the lily. But it wasn't sadness for Jill, or for Bryn, who, after all, had accepted his caregiving role, one choice among the limited options he faced, yet with its own incentives. He was doing all he could for this woman he loved, and that was something, more than most people had.

Ella thought about her own choices and how she had ended up here. It didn't feel like something she had chosen. Certainly it wasn't the most she was capable of, sitting in this wooden chair, blocking the front door; the problem was that every competing offer involved worse work for comparable pay. Reluctantly, her mind dipped into her decision to leave graduate school, like a harried parent poking down the back of a diaper to see if it was wet. Leaving hadn't felt like a choice, not really. This was tired ground to reexamine, and to what end? She wasn't going back. Suddenly, the years stretched out in front of her, the hand working its way around the clock, first this one, and then the next clock, in the next living room. Next year she would be thirty. This wasn't the life she had imagined for herself.

Ella heard the key in the lock and scrambled to put her chair back before the door swung open. Bryn strode in smiling, a paper bag of groceries in each hand. "Stay for tea?" he asked over his shoulder as he walked into the kitchen.

• 7 •

It was after sunset, and Ella and Alix were walking around Lake Harriet with ice cream cones in hand. It was a perfect July evening for lake walking, warm, with wind that kept the mosquitoes at bay, and, for a moment, Ella felt wonderfully content looking out across the water.

"I ran into Jenny today," Ella said. "That girl I babysat when I was a teenager."

"Yeah?" Alix said, only half paying attention. "How's she?"

"Oh, fine," Ella said. "She's at, like, St. Thomas now, studying marketing or something. She asked me what I'm doing."

"Yeah?" Alix said.

"I said I take care of elderly people, and she said, 'Oh, now I feel bad.'"

No one had ever said explicitly that to Ella before, it felt like a frank version of what she was always hearing—"How wonderful. I could never do what you do." Jenny had smiled at her, looking remarkably beautiful, sun-kissed with bare shoulders, wearing delicate sandals, holding only her car keys. And Ella had stood there, absurdly burdened with library books and groceries and all the objects deemed vital or potentially useful for her day. She had hauled it all to and from work on the bus, flat-footed in cheap men's sandals, suitable for cleaning Sharon's bathroom. If Jenny felt bad, Ella felt worse: old, tired, disappointed.

"Let's move to Europe," Alix said, as she sometimes did, only this cheerful bit of pretending failed to buoy Ella's mood this time. She flopped onto the bench where Alix had just settled.

"I've decided to apply for that residency in Spain," Alix added, a little bashfully.

Ella was startled but didn't want to be discouraging.

"I told you I think you should. Still, you know I can't come. With what portfolio would I apply?" Ella dabbled in her creative pursuits, a drawing or painting sketched in but incomplete, a poem, an essay, and then six months of browsing interior design magazines, reading novels, hours of creative energy devoted to elaborate meals and rearranging everything in their apartment, whereas Alix tore into her art like a dog with a rawhide chew, nearly every day, no matter how long her shift at the coffee shop proved to be. Somehow it didn't make Ella feel bad, Alix's talent and the modest beginnings of recognition thereof. Alix's talent inspired Ella. But Alix's discipline she did covet for herself, deeply, even a little bitterly.

"You could come as an au pair," Alix said, rising from the bench and stretching.

"I think I'd rather sit with Jill, thanks," Ella said.

She'd considered it, now and again, but

the rewards of an exotic location seemed scant compared to the effort caring for the children of wealthy parents would require. The more elder care Ella did, the less appealing child care became. The naps were so much shorter, the falls and diaper changes so much more frequent. Ella tended to favor the easy and safe, and increasingly, she feared, the familiar.

"Go without me," she said. "I'll find a roommate."

"I'll hear back in December," Alix said. "Then we can talk about it."

As they resumed walking, Ella pictured the nine months without Alix unhappily. She would miss her terribly to be certain, though it also seemed so tedious, to be left with the inconvenience of living with a roommate, of continuing the plodding pace of her life while hearing, from a distance, about the novelty of Alix's. If it was hard not to get discouraged now, how much worse, she realized, it could become. Actually, Ella was being too optimistic. She was focusing on her inconvenience and her jealousy without fully considering the solitude. Ella was an independent person, but she acknowledged, in reluctant, wistful little moments of melancholy, that Alix was the only thing in her life that couldn't be improved upon.

Their relationship had begun by exceeding her hopes for what friendship could bring, and then it had surpassed her erotic and romantic fantasies, for before Alix, Ella had generally preferred the wanting to the having, the ache of appetite over fumbling attempts at satiety. Similarly, Ella liked to imagine going on trips, even liked to plan them, but didn't really like to go, because what if she ran out of money? What if she got lost? What if it was tiring and expensive and disappointing, and someone stole her wallet, and the weather was terrible, and she missed her train? So much better, safer, to imagine the trip as she might like for it to unfold, to feel the surge of excitement, of possibility. Though she also knew that fantasies of travel and seduction were masturbatory exercises in nostalgia, revisiting, time and again, the imaginary scaffolding that still stood, conveniently, in place: here are the cobbled streets of an ancient city, here are the pastries filled with marzipan, here is the surf breaking on the sand; or here he or she is, wanting me just as I have always longed to be wanted, settling that most exquisitely painful of questions, probing that most erotically charged of all tender, abused places: Do I deserve to be wanted? Am I good enough to love?

With Alix, all of these hollow fantasies seemed childish and boring, for even though they were tailored to what Ella believed she wanted, they never taught her anything new about what else there might be to want. Alix had kicked aside the dream set that had stood in place since adolescence and stirred up Ella's romantic imagination with marvelous unpredictability. To Ella's surprise, it was the imperfections that most improved upon the fantasies; it was the ways they were able to hurt each other, and comfort each other, that made it all real, made the stakes feel as though they mattered. The more Ella knew of Alix's flaws, the more fiercely she loved her, the more she practically shook with the desire to protect her, to meet each need she was able to whether petty or profound. Whenever Alix bought the wrong thing, was tempted by some product's flashy label or sly illusion of a "deal," Ella would sigh crossly and watch Alix's pride in her savvy purchase slip into wariness. Ella would feel a cutting guilt over having so easily deflated Alix's minor happiness, but it was more painful still to picture Alix navigating the world with such dangerous innocence. Ella would think, with determination, **I must** always **be here to take care of her.** When she imagined Alix as a beautiful, gray-haired woman of seventy, she pictured the skin on her elbows roughish, puckered, loose, and the feminine vulnerability it would reveal made Ella want to kiss those future imaginary elbows worshipfully, made her want to cry with love and fear of death.

The things Ella had imagined she wanted in a long-term lover seemed so insignificant, so recycled compared to what Alix offered. She had thought that she wanted someone masculine of center because she had learned to eroticize power, but Alix was utterly a girl, not just in her lithe, curving body or her pretty clothes but in her self-deprecation, her naïveté, her easy, unembarrassed tears. Ella had thought she wanted someone possessing expansively cultivated expertise, that she might always learn from them. Alix was yet too young for any sort of expansive expertise, but her curiosity was exhilarating, exasperating, and, best of all, infectious. Ella had thought she wanted someone self-assured, so that their choosing of her would feel like a solid affirmation of her worth. Alix's lack of self-assurance meant Ella was more interested in loving her life-affirmingly than in checking to see what receiving Alix's love proved about herself. It was like sitting down with a menu and looking for the ingredients you knew you liked—sweet red peppers, the bite of citrus, savory bacon—and then finding more pleasure in anise, tamarind, cardamom. The best part wasn't the novelty of the flavors but the feeling that if **this** surprise can bring me such pleasure, what other delights might yet be found in unexpected pairings?

· 8 ·

Ella locked her bike to her usual street sign and rang the doorbell. When it failed to draw a response, she circled the house to investigate the backyard. As she peeked around the corner, she saw Bryn sitting in a burst of sun. His body appeared lazy with contentment, although fatigue was more probably what had caused his limbs to spread loosely, his head to tilt back. He was smoking a cigarette, something Ella had never seen him do. Normally Ella found smoking distasteful, but there was something so beautiful and unstudied in his pose, the sun on his upturned face, the tendril of smoke escaping sensually from his mouth. The strain was gone from his body, at least momentarily, and Ella luxuriated in the sight. He looked, for a moment, like a much younger man, and this illusion of youth wrung Ella's heart. Turning his head he caught sight of her, and she tried to muster a friendly smile, hoping the expression on her face hadn't been condescending in its sympathy and pleasure.

"Hello," he called out cheerfully, and gestured to the empty chair that faced those he and Jill occupied. Ella dropped into the seat with exaggerated relief, her tote bag flung aside, her knees pulled to her chest. The weather was magnificent, they agreed, coasting between the oppressive heat of summer and the warning downtempo of fall. As they chatted, Ella felt with growing determination that it was past time she corrected the male pronouns he used to refer to Alix. She would say something today. Now. But her speeding pulse gave her pause, made her wincingly, blushingly, look away. It felt like that surge of dread that so often preceded announcing one's gayness to the unsuspecting. That was exactly what this was, of course, for she wasn't outing Alix as female but herself as female-partnered.

She soothed herself internally. **No hurry,** she thought, even as a nauseating sense of urgency thrummed through her. **I'll just tell him like it's funny it's taken me this long, I can just say, I don't know why I haven't told you, or it's a hazard of the trade, it's become habitual not to mention such things at work, or I've been meaning to tell you, Alix is a woman.** She shifted uneasily in her seat. **It's no big deal!** she all but shouted at herself. But the butterflies filled her stomach, rushed up into her throat, blocked the words from spilling out. She changed tactics, albeit only with herself. **He doesn't need to know,** she thought. **What business is it of his? He doesn't want to know, probably. Doesn't want the accompanying mental images of what I might do in bed, with whom. Might prefer we don't acknowledge the whole bedroom thing.**

Bryn wasn't attracted to Ella, she felt safe

in assuming, though at times he showed a hint of swagger around her, not sexual posturing, just a bearing that read as **Don't doubt that I am still a** man, **not yet an old codger.** Ella's (generally affirming) response to Bryn's masculinity necessarily factored into her relationship with him, and prompted concern about how his knowledge of her queerness would shrink the dimensions of the already relatively narrow field in which they knew how to relate to each other. Not just because of the predictable gender roles—Bryn smiling his easy grin, advising her on home repairs—but because he assumed that she and Alix were more like he and Jill had been than they could ever truly be.

She felt that this was at the heart of her hesitation. She believed he took some comfort in imagining Alix and her as earlier versions of himself and Jill, a young couple in love, short on funds, building a life. All of which was technically true, while shielding from view the untidy vitality of their differences. Even for the sorts of gay folks who wanted access to a traditional union, family, home, there was the difference of seeking access versus the privilege of perceiving it, unquestionably, as birthright. Besides, Ella wasn't that sort of gay anyway. She didn't want to get married. She didn't want to have children. She didn't want to own a house. She actually thought it smacked of the **ordinary,** her having fallen in love and paired off, but these weren't the sorts of things she could see herself telling Bryn. It wouldn't just come across as vaguely disappointing, but also, perhaps, like a critique of his values, which, in a way, it was. She did admire him, though. He was almost painfully admirable, in his dedicated caregiving, in his contained, unfathomable love and suffering. Lisa, Nick's wife, had called him "a good man, **too** good," and Ella, though brought up in the "We Are All Sinners" school of thought, felt inclined to agree. Why didn't this thought move her more? Why didn't she sigh over him like a housewife watching a Lifetime weepie? Then again, Ella had always been more moved by imperfect love.

Still. Ella didn't worry that Alix would leave her for a man, one who would fuck her full of the babies she longed for, or that Alix would leave her for an impossibly chic sort of woman, irresistibly seductive. She seldom worried about Alix leaving her, period, though on the rare occasions when she did, this was the flavor of her worry: Alix would leave her for someone who was **good**. A **better** sort of person, one less greedy for attention, one who welcomed the blinders of faithfulness, rather than barely tolerating them, as Ella did. Someone lacking in the abhorrent, compulsive narcissism that drew Ella to mirrors and cameras and the admiring glances of strangers like a punishing enchantment. Ella was ashamed of how her own beauty comforted and seduced her; she visited it like a secret lover, she stroked it softly like a young boy watching television, one hand tucked into his pajama bottoms, fondling his small, flaccid treasure. She despised her excess weight with a bitterness that sometimes tipped into violence. As a teenager, she had tried to starve it off, tried to burn it off, running under the scorching heat of the noonday sun, as though only tremendous discomfort would prove to her body the seriousness of her intentions. Sometimes, she slapped it, left angry handprints on the shivering white curves of her belly, clawed red stripes into the dimpled flesh of her inner thighs.

Nothing worked, of course. She was always at least a little bit plump, and, in time, she came to feel almost grateful for it, aware of how narrowly she had missed a life where her vanity might have surged to meet the boundaries of her selfhood. Ella was a sensualist who fought vicious, doomed battles with her natural appetites, who yearned to become an ascetic; as Eleanor Roosevelt had reportedly longed to be beautiful, Ella longed to be good, and if a part of her wanted to distance itself from the bourgeois predictability of Bryn and

Jill's pre-accident life, another part of her was loath to dash Bryn's illusions of wholesome, middling solidarity. Perhaps, for a bit longer, she could impersonate a daughter he might wish to have had, one perpetually modest, loyal, wise.

· 9 ·

Jill's cousin Tina is visiting from Iowa," Bryn informed Ella as he let her into the house. "She's at the store now, buying some vitamins she thinks Jill should be taking." This was a cue that, for the moment, they could speak frankly.

"How's all that going?" Ella asked, with a cautious hint of skepticism, for she heard the undertone of critique in Bryn's voice, recognized it from some of their conversations about Nick. It didn't occur to her that he might talk about her with Nick in this way, too ("Ella cut your mom's toenails today, but of course I had to **ask**"), for she assumed that the murmuring of sympathy was **her** role and hers alone. With this invitation to grouse, he said, "Oh, well enough. She's coming up with a new errand to run every ten minutes or so. It just kills her to sit with Jill for very long."

Ella could see both sides of this, she'd seen it before, when other clients had relatives visit. It was jarring, the decline, and they felt guilty about how rarely they came, and also eager for it to be over. Presumably they were there to see the impaired loved one, but it was so difficult to know how to act, how to pass time with someone only partially aware, partially coherent. This would be harder than was typical with Jill, for there would be no semblance of conversation, most likely not even a sign that she recognized her cousin. Tina would feel compelled to demonstrate the usefulness of her visit; she wouldn't understand that sitting with Jill would provide Bryn with tremendously welcome relief, and would also better fulfill the presumed purpose of coming to see her cousin. It likely didn't occur to her that these errands could be read as a criticism of Bryn's competence.

Still, Bryn probably understood each of these variables, although it would be hard for him to bring Ella's level of objectivity to the situation.

When Tina strode in, complaining about the pharmacy, Ella could see why he was disinclined to muster much empathy. Tina wasn't insufferable, but she was annoying. She acted as though Jill were a baby and she an experienced mother, come to bestow her wisdom upon an incompetent father and babysitter, when, actually, she knew little of the situation, of the years that Bryn had handled these reins with deft assurance weighted with grief, of the months of meticulous observation Ella had clocked. She made bold observations of the obvious as though this proved something about her sensitivity. "She mutters," she observed, as though this were really a keen insight, and "She's lost weight." "Yes," Ella agreed. "She has," Bryn confirmed. They didn't need to exchange a glance, their shared rustle of irritation that bordered on amusement was fully synchronized, as if they sat side by side on the same beach, felt the same cold wave lap their bare feet.

It was a small, discreet pleasure, this silently united front, even though Ella was prepared to defend Tina later, to try to soften Bryn's annoyance. That changed when Tina, getting ready to leave again, began to give Ella orders.

"All of the rooms could use vacuuming," Tina said. "Also Jill's teeth need brushing and her fingernails need trimming and the bed could use fresh sheets. And there's quite a bit of laundry to wash, and the dishwasher needs to be unloaded. The kitchen sink needs scouring, and so does the stovetop. There should be plenty to keep you occupied."

Ella nodded but could scarcely believe how high-handed this was; she had never been in a situation quite like it. Bryn registered no surprise, but after Tina left, he said, gently, as if by way of apology, "You answer to me." Still, with furious reluctance, Ella completed each task on the list. She wouldn't give Tina any cause to complain about Bryn's choice of caregiver or how he managed **the help**. Part of Ella's fury was rooted in laziness, in her distaste for additional, unanticipated duties, although the more significant part of it sprung from a buried suspicion that she ought to be doing more, that Bryn would never ask her to do as much as she should, as much as he truly needed. Sometimes she would halfheartedly offer to wash the dishes, and he would tell her not to, but she knew the greater kindness would be to simply do them without giving him a chance to object.

Once she and Jill were alone, Ella tried to decide whether to tackle Jill's grooming first or last. Jill was calm now and certainly wouldn't remain so through the clipping of her nails or the attempt, likely futile, to brush her teeth. That could make focusing Ella's attention on other tasks much more difficult afterward. On the other hand, it would be satisfying to have the jobs completed **and** Jill calm when Bryn and Tina returned, a much more likely possibility if Jill had hours to recover. Or maybe it would be better not to give the illusion that all of this had been accomplished too easily.

Ella started to get the vacuum and then thought the noise might upset Jill; better to group it with the other upsetting tasks. Jill was washing her baby doll in the bathroom sink now, so she might remain occupied for a while longer. Ella headed into the kitchen warily. She almost never left Jill alone longer than it took to use the bathroom and wasn't sure what to expect, although surely Bryn did this all the time.

The afternoon sun poured in through the window over the dirty porcelain sink. On the windowsill a few avocado pits hung suspended by toothpicks over glass jam jars filled with water, their submerged roots branching like pale veins. A small cut-crystal orb dangling from fishing line hooked on the window clasp refracted sunlight spotted across the room, across Ella's chest and belly, probably across her face, although she couldn't see her reflection. She imagined she could feel points of warmth on her cheeks and forehead and lips, adorning her hair with haphazard brightness. She looked under the sink and found, with some digging, an old can of Bon Ami and a worn scrub brush. The mesh drain catcher was full of unrecognizable bits of food, which Ella emptied into the compost bucket, though its surface remained opaquely coated once she was done. She set the drain catcher on the counter and began to sprinkle the Bon Ami all over the sink. She knew that by the time she was done scrubbing, the belly of her shirt would be soaked, and she wondered if the cleaning powder would bleach it. Still, it wasn't like it was a cherished garment. Belatedly she realized it would have been better to soak the components of the stove's gas burners **before** cleaning the sink. Oh well, she would soak them in the dishpan—but then she would need to clean the dishpan without dirtying the newly scrubbed porcelain. Meanwhile, she strained to hear the bathroom sink, Jill's jabbering and splashing. She thought she could make out the sound of the faucet, but that alone didn't confirm Jill's engagement with it. Ella wiped her angry-skinned hands on a dirty dish towel and went to investigate.

Eventually all of the tasks had been more or less completed except for vacuuming the rooms in Jill's immediate vicinity and dealing with her teeth and nails. Jill was kneeling in the middle of the den, placing objects and towels in a laundry basket and removing them, an imitation of someone sorting. She didn't seem to have been bothered by the muffled roar of the vacuum in the more distant rooms, but then Ella hadn't been present to see if it had registered in Jill's face or demeanor while it was actively occurring. Now Ella stood and considered her next step. Her impulse was to finish the vacuuming, logically complete one job before beginning the next, but brushing Jill's teeth and trimming her nails required a degree of cooperation that vacuuming didn't. Cooperation was unlikely anyway, although possibly slightly more likely if Jill

wasn't already rattled when they began—
the element of surprise had proven useful
in the past.

Ella was sweaty but not yet tired; she still
had vestiges of adrenaline from the cleaning, which she would lose if she sat down
for even a short break. In compromise she
instead remained standing, turned to look
out the window, felt the ceiling fan stir the
damp curls on her neck beneath the messy
knot of hair tied on the top of her head.
The windows looked out over the backyard
and its trees and their long late-afternoon
shadows. Ella considered that she would
rather be mowing that yard with the old
push mower so she could turn totally
inward, listen to poetry read aloud on her
headphones, feel the sun on her skin and
smell the cut grass. Of course that would
be impossible when home alone with Jill.

Ella heard the front door open just as
she approached Jill with the damp and
foamy toothbrush Bryn had indicated was
once hers; he didn't bother to pretend tooth
brushing occurred with any regularity, even

with Tina listening. Ella paused to determine whether it was Bryn or Tina, for only Bryn would understand that the inevitable screaming and struggle wouldn't be Ella's fault. She decided it was Tina because Bryn would have hollered hello even if he had groceries to put away. Ella hesitated further. She didn't want to sound or appear unoccupied with her work incomplete, but she had already resolved that she wouldn't fight Jill with Tina present. She put the toothbrush back and went to plug in the vacuum.

The trouble was, Ella was unaccustomed to having a job that didn't fill her with even a small dose of dread, that involved almost no objectionable tasks, and now that she'd found one, it was hard to give it up. Ella hated cleaning, she had wanted to transition into a purely companion role for many years, but most people, like Sharon, wanted a companion who was also a drudge. It was unusual in the Midwest for middle-class folks of Bryn's generation to hire a housekeeper. It was unclear to Ella if this was entirely a financial consideration or the principle of cleaning one's own messes in a culture that deeply valued humility. Either way, Ella was the only one professionally cleaning in any of the homes where she worked, and in the early years of her caregiving career she was almost impossibly conscientious. She never so much as left a water glass in the sink, and if her client took a nap, she sought some way to busy herself, looking longingly at the newspaper folded open to the crossword puzzle, succumbing only once everything was impeccably tidy. Now that her only clear tasks involved preventing Jill from leaving, destroying anything valuable, or hurting herself, as well as occasional help with dressing and grooming, Ella focused her attention on Bryn, when he was home, and passing the time when he wasn't.

One day, Nick's wife, Lisa, had come to drop off some paperwork for Bryn and found Ella alone with Jill, staring listlessly into space, watching the clock tick through the minutes. She had gone out to her car and come back with an old issue of

Vanity Fair, as though Ella's boredom were an unsafe working condition and OSHA required them to provide reading materials. Ella had been grateful for the gesture and, more especially, the precedent. She began to bring things to do: a bit of mending, a novel, a book of poems, a sketch pad, her journal. Getting ready for work became like packing for a long and uneventful journey, but Ella felt a need not to flaunt her amusements, not just because it suggested she could handle more responsibilities but, worse, because it suggested that the work was so absurdly easy anyone could do it. Was that true? Could anyone do it? It was certainly the best job Ella had ever had, initially because she was paid to talk to Bryn, who had become her friend, someone she would happily talk to anyway, and now with the incredible bonus that she could read and, also, write.

She drew Jill, and wrote poems about her. She drew the birch trees in the front yard, and the fir trees in the back, and the elegantly simple coffee table Bryn had designed and built, and she wished that she could draw Bryn's dear, craggy features. She wished she could draw his sadness, only that was far beyond her skill, it would look maudlin, cartoonish, whereas in real life, it was like a shadow that passed over his smile. Whenever she heard the front door, she tucked her things away, as though tidying up for company or preparing to leave, but really, she was embarrassed that this was how she earned her wages.

One day Nick came and stayed. "Our washer's broken," he explained, toting in a giant bag of laundry. He watched TV in between loads, passing Ella and Jill during each rotation. Ella wasn't sure how to behave with him around, what did he think her role was? It seemed like needless self-punishment to sit unoccupied, and yet, would he frown upon her reading? Ella pulled out a section of the newspaper, determined not to make this into too big of a deal, but when his footsteps approached, she pretended to herself that she had lost interest, tucking the newspaper, defiantly still visible, between her bag and the sofa. It was the same the next time she heard his footsteps, and he paused before her and said, "You don't have to hide it. I know you've got a newspaper. I don't care if you read." This made Ella angry, almost more angry than if he had forbidden her to read, for if he didn't object, why did he need to humiliate her? To display his power to decide **whether** it was okay? It seemed cruel without any practical agenda. If Ella weren't so embarrassed, she might have recognized this as the frankness she had admired in him when they'd first met, or even as a kindness, that she might read without interruption, but her cheeks still burned when she remembered it a month, two months later.

She always left the newspaper for Bryn, his potential interest in it kept her subscribing even when she sought corners to cut, because he had once said he missed it, confessed with a wistfulness he seldom showed. She didn't think he read it, really, it seemed he couldn't focus on much of anything with

Say Say Say

Jill messing about, grabbing things from his hands, finding liquids to pour out and solids to crumple. Since these interruptions didn't prevent Ella from resuming her reading once they were resolved, she assumed there was more to it than that, though she didn't allow herself to put the obvious name to it, which was, of course, depression.

This job Ella had been doing for years, it was pink-collar, no doubt about it; it was utterly, overwhelmingly, women's work. She sliced sandwiches on white bread into four neat triangles, and she ironed handkerchiefs, and she baked dozens and dozens of cookies. She stripped and made beds, singles, doubles, kings and queens, and some liked the sheets tucked in at the end of the bed so nothing migrated as they tossed and turned, and some liked the sheets untucked so they could move, but no one was shy about letting Ella know their preference. Ella also polished shoes, sewed on missing buttons, and switched out winter and summer clothes as the seasons changed, only to switch them back again, and she made meat loaf that got eaten and salads that didn't, and she cut gruesome toenails with cheerful composure, and shaved men's faces, and even one woman's legs. ("I feel so feminine now!" the woman had declared, joyfully.) She bathed men and women alike, which was sensitive, slippery work, but less difficult than convincing them to shower at all. She changed enormous disposable briefs, heavy with urine so dark it was almost brown, and wiped poorly cleaned bottoms with damp cloths pinched between gloved fingers.

Caregiving work was women's work, and yet Bryn did it without question. He and Nick, strapping men over six feet tall, would hose Jill down together once a week in the shower while she screamed bloody murder. He cooked her meals and washed her clothes, and felt her forehead to see if she had a fever, and selected her outfits from the now-stained and newly ill-fitting assortment that remained from her former life. When Ella entered the scene, she took pleasure in selecting new clothes at the thrift store for her, and she and Bryn would marvel, once they got home, at how different size 6 jeans could be, depending on the brand. Bryn and Ella and Jill would sit at the kitchen table and sip their tea, or, in Jill's case, gulp and abandon it, or plunge her hand into it. They would talk about the best way to grill eggplant or the ideal way to boil an egg, and whether Jill had recently had a bowel movement, and speculate if there was a dentist, anywhere, who would brave the horrors of Jill's decaying mouth.

From Bryn, over the months, Ella learned that it needed to be hot to grow good tomatoes, and that the only grapefruits worth eating were from Texas, and how to differentiate cedar planks from pine. She also learned that a man could demonstrate his love for a woman with the alert practicality and dutiful nurturing Ella had only ever observed the other way around. It so moved and surprised Ella that she was forced to wonder why. Undoubtedly other men found themselves in similar roles, but the abstract love of strangers had meant little to Ella, while this love she observed so intimately it was almost as though she absorbed its warmth. Why was this so startling? Did she think so little of men that it surprised her when they displayed the decency she would expect from a woman? Or did she think so little of women that they didn't warrant tender, self-sacrificing care from a man? It was both. It was neither. Together, Bryn and Jill swung quiet, graceful blows to a secret suspicion of hers, one she had nurtured through the years: that men's romantic love for women was, at best, improbable.

This sour little grimace of a theory wasn't one Ella had lost much sleep over. She had liked and wanted both men and women often enough over the years, and, often enough, they had liked and wanted her, but in the end, it had been Alix's love that mattered, and hypothetical love between heterosexuals had become something uninteresting to spend much time thinking about, at least until now. Newly confronted with her prejudice, she sent an exploratory feeler into the why of it, or maybe, more accurately, the when. She couldn't really remember a time before she knew that being female put her on the fringes of things. In elementary school, the figurative boys' club that seemed to sit in the center of life was endlessly tantalizing—what were they doing in there? Why wasn't she invited? But it wasn't until adolescence that she began to feel the anemia, the slow, internal bleed of shame that still left her pallid and diminished. When had the ulcer begun? Perhaps at ten, when she and her best guy friend, Tim, had been joyfully hollering and roughhousing with the youth pastor and her mother had pulled her aside, whispering, "You're too old now to wrestle with grown men." Perhaps when Tim, a secret double agent, had reported back from the boys' club at school, "Jeremiah told all the guys that your boobs are nice and big and it's a shame you're too fat." That had been when she was twelve. By thirteen, she expected to be sexualized with a gleeful kind of disgust, glances and comments equal parts hunger and disparagement. By college she was accustomed to the jocks who mocked her with blearily drunken venom even as they propositioned her, bloodshot eyes already removing her dress with clumsy violence, and the more insidious damage of, at twenty-three, being courted by an attractive, charming man who only ever wanted to see her in the privacy of his apartment.

None of that was the worst of it. The worst of it, as Ella saw it, was not knowing what bits of her psyche were herself and what bits were scar tissue, and also, of not knowing how to circumvent the damage done to her own sexual wiring. Was Ella naturally kind and gentle, or had the culture made her so, worn her down like beach glass, pushed her to her knees, forever eager to please? Why could she feel sexy—even with a woman—only with her breasts pushed forward and her hips tipped back, a sultry pout on her pretty face? That was all learned, of course, but it seemed it couldn't be unlearned, Ella had tried, and trying had only rendered her emotionally frayed and sexually closed. If Ella couldn't untangle any of this, how could anyone else hope to? Even the men who had believed they loved her, what was it that they had loved? The supplicating Ella on her knees? The teasing pout, poised to wrap around their cocks? There were no threads to parse for the authentic self; even a critique of her supplicating pose was a form of misogyny, as far as Ella was concerned, for who was any man to criticize the person she now couldn't help but be? It was a hopeless state of affairs. It was, at best, an improbable love.

Enter Bryn's love for Jill. Routinely now he fished her turds out of the bathtub, he held her close when she wept, despite the smell of death that continually wafted from her neglected gums. He loved her in a hopeless way, and he showed it through the Sisyphean tasks of her daily care. It changed Ella, in a small but significant way. It didn't make her less angry, although it funneled the scope of her anger.

Something shifted there, some distance became smaller, some wound still failed to heal yet ceased to be nursed with quite the same glittering-eyed mistrust. She began to feel that perhaps she and Alix were not so different from Bryn and Jill after all. Part of what stirred Ella's tenderness for Alix's future, aging self was a resentful anticipation of the sexual scorn of men, of the invisibility aging women experienced, yet here was Bryn, patiently tending the haggard physical shell of the young woman he had married decades before. There was no practiced performance of femininity required of Jill, no masterful erotic agenda being imposed by Bryn. Their roles were stripped genderless through a wildfire of loss, standing stark where lush growth might have hidden predators, there was only charred and shivering sufferer and co-sufferer, lover and beloved.

Ella's bike broke on her way to work: the flat of the pedal snapped off, leaving only the rounded metal pin it had spun on. She could still ride it, but it was clumsy, dangerous going, her shoe slid forward and back over the pin as if she were trying to scrape it clean, and it became doubly indulgent to coast down hills, without the strain of momentum or the treacherous movement of her foot.

When she arrived, she told Bryn immediately, as if he were her mother and therefore best involved in any sort of problem-solving from the get-go. He strode over to her bike like a father to an automobile with a mysterious leak, a quarter concerned, a quarter disapproving, half eager to get his hands dirty fixing something. There was little he could do without a new pedal, however, and he soon rejoined Ella and Jill inside.

"They might have something at the bike co-op," Bryn said. "They let you fix bikes there for free, they have parts, tools." Ella looked at him with polite doubt. Was she going to ride a broken bike there as the sun set when her shift ended? Would she know what to do with the tools? Clearly not.

"We can throw it in the back of the truck," Bryn said. "You can sit with Jill, and I can go in and check things out." The **rightness** of this solution filled Ella with relief, though the circumstances made her hesitant. She was there to work for Bryn, but here he was, offering the time up to work for her. She sensed it would be embarrassing for him if she phrased her concerns so baldly, especially since she intended to accept his offer. Instead of her usual, mother-instilled habit of declining hospitality twice before accepting—"Oh no, I couldn't possibly take any of your cake. Oh, absolutely I'm certain, but thank you so much for offering. Well, perhaps, if you insist, but only a taste"—she jumped straight into shy, heartfelt gratitude. "Oh, that would be so sweet, if you really wouldn't mind." They swapped Jill's tattered slippers for shoes and piled into the truck, bike in the back, Jill firmly sandwiched in the middle, not at all where she thought she belonged. Jill loved to sit in the truck, or perhaps **love** wasn't the word, for what did any of them know of her pleasures or motives these days? She often slipped into the passenger seat of the parked but unlocked truck and shut the door, leaving Bryn and Ella chatting in the yard. Was she cold? Was she trying to ensure that Bryn couldn't leave without her? Did she think she had somewhere to go? There was no way of knowing, no one to ask.

Each time the three of them got into the truck, it was the same struggle to move Jill out of the passenger seat that had always been hers. Of course, Ella could have sat in the middle, for Jill had never tried to open the car door when it was moving, and she had ready access to the handle whenever Ella wasn't with her, but no one seriously considered this. It would have been too awkward, squished together shoulder to shoulder, thigh to thigh, Bryn's hand moving against Ella's knee every time he shifted gears. Just **not** seriously considering it was a little tense, actually; Bryn didn't look at Ella as he pleaded and prodded to get Jill to scoot over, a note of urgency creeping into his soothing tone, with Ella standing at a slight distance, arms crossed, as though this had nothing to do with her, Bryn and Ella both afraid Ella would finally, reluctantly, offer to sit bitch.

When they got to the bike co-op parking lot, Bryn swung out of the driver's seat and lifted Ella's clunky bike out of the truck bed with a careful ease that seemed at odds with the bike's heaviness. This dissonance struck Ella as somehow representative of the whole situation. She would have been shy to bring any bike into the co-op, but the unloveliness of the one she had would not have been the reason. It was, however, the reason she was embarrassed for Bryn, in his simple, broken-in button-down and beautifully frayed jeans, and the plain gold band that was his wedding ring. What had this cheap, shabby women's bike to do with him? **Kindness,** she thought, and that stilled her fretting, or at least the abstract dimension of it, for Jill grew increasingly distracting beside her.

It seemed like ages had passed since she'd watched Bryn wheel in through the front door across the lot, but then, at last, he came out and strode toward them, empty-handed. He reported back to Ella with a pessimism that was almost cheerful, like a plumber telling you how very dire and expensive your problem is, although glad for the job just the same. He had been digging through their enormous bin of used pedals, looking for the right type that would also attach to the correct side. No luck yet, but he would keep at it. He seemed invigorated by the challenge, and Ella sensed he liked the masculine camaraderie of the co-op, broad-knuckled hands dark with grease, guys giving each other a good-natured hard time just for the hell of it.

Ella kept Jill inside the truck for as long as she possibly could, not that it was either easy or pleasant. They were parked in the shade but the air felt close in the small cab, even with the windows cracked. Jill squirmed and muttered, "And why? And why? Go go go go. And you have to tell them. Mine. Mine."

"Bryn will be back soon," Ella soothed, uncertain if Jill even knew she was addressing her, since they were sitting side by side, so that it was even harder than usual to make eye contact. "He's just fixing my bike—it won't take very long. He'll be right back, and then we'll go home."

"Get out. And I don't want to. And I don't want to." Jill unbuckled her seat belt and reached for the driver's-side door handle as Ella stretched across her to lock the door. Ella knew Jill would eventually remember how to unlock it again, and she considered how if Jill were a small child watching her lock the door it would likely cue her in on what must be done to unlock it. As it was, cause and effect seemed mysterious to Jill; she seemed to exist in a reality where actions—including her own—were completely unrelated to one another, each floating in time in its own sealed vacuum. Jill flipped and flipped the door handle; she scrabbled her hands over the surface of the door, across the window crank and the map in the pocket. Eventually her finger caught under the lock and flipped it up, but Ella pressed it down before Jill's hand made it back to the handle. It clearly agitated her that Ella was sitting so close, only Ella needed to be able to reach the lock.

She shifted her body so that her attention seemed focused away from Jill, out the windshield and toward the trees that sheltered them. She kept her arm snaked discreetly behind Jill without touching her and wondered how long she could possibly sit there poised to press the lock. She was grateful Jill hadn't figured out how to honk the horn, though of course it could happen at any moment, and then what? Jill shifted her attention to rattling the air vents with irritated purposefulness, ignoring the turn signal arm and radio dials. She glared at Ella and twisted as far from her as she could. It was unpleasant to feel so disliked. Ella tried speaking soothingly again, "Bryn will be back any minute, and then we'll go home. He'll be right back, I promise." Ella didn't even know if Bryn's name meant anything to Jill but she hoped her tone conveyed reassurance, suggested she and Jill weren't in opposition.

Ella's arm began to ache, and she considered her options. Jill was happy enough to sit in the truck at home; perhaps if she were alone in the cab, she would settle in. Ella slid across the seat to the passenger door and opened it quickly, hopping out and immediately swinging it shut. She decided to stand back just barely out of Jill's sight line, even though it left both door handles unguarded.

If this worked at all, it was only for a little bit, because it seemed barely moments had

passed before Ella was forced to lean against
the door on the driver's side to keep Jill
from slipping out. Jill complained loudly,
her voice sharp but not panicked, "What!
What! And it's mine! And it's mine! Go! Go!
Go! And go! What!" Ella felt as though she
were going about this all wrong, as though
someone who wasn't her would know how
to placate and distract. Force seemed like
such a last resort, so bullyish and lazy, and
Ella almost felt as though she shared in Jill's
disgust for this lumbering, awkward girl
leaning rude and heavy against the truck's
hot and dusty metal. Perhaps they ought to
take a little walk along the edge of the small
pond behind the co-op.

Ella opened the door. "Should we go
for a walk? Come on, Jill," she said, and
she stepped aside with a gesture of invitation. How do you walk with someone who
doesn't want to walk with you? You follow
them, and when you want them to turn
you step in front of them, hoping they start
avoiding you in another direction. This was
not a foolproof system, but somehow they

jerked strangely across the side of the lot to the path by the pond. Ella felt fortunate that Jill didn't seem interested in leaving the path; she only seemed intent on avoiding Ella, and so they made their way slowly in the same direction, with Ella trailing.

The water looked murky and the September sun was hot on the goose-shit-smeared tar, but the breeze off the water was cool and pleasant. Did Jill feel her sweat-dampened hair lift and ruffle pleasingly off her neck and temples as Ella did? Could she observe the sunlight on the rippling water, the movement of the grass below and the branches above? Both her posture and her muttering still communicated only distress. Ella began to wonder if they were getting too far for Bryn to easily spot them should he discover the truck sitting empty. There was a bench beside a weeping willow just ahead that looked inviting but Ella couldn't imagine convincing Jill to sit beside her, even for a very short time.

Reluctantly she sped up, stepping in front of Jill, who then angrily backed away before turning around and moving in the general direction of the parking lot. Having a destination instead of merely ambling proved much more difficult to strategize toward; Ella had to curtail Jill's listing and turning by menacing bodily in all the directions that didn't lead to the lot. Eventually, though, they neared the truck. Unfortunately, Jill was not interested in resuming her captivity, instead making her way toward the construction site that sprawled on the parking lot's far side. This was so stressful it was almost unreal. Ella's hands and the small of her back were wet with sweat. She tried to corral Jill with a new desperation, but Jill was like a frightened animal, thwarted in her will, and she snarled and yelled and dodged with kinetic illogic, sprinting onto the dirty boards laid over a deep construction-related gully.

"Hey! No!" yelled a concerned man in a hard hat, his exclamations followed by a torrent of worried Spanish. Ella grabbed Jill's wrist and yanked, and Jill bellowed and fought, teetering over the gully. The man with the hard hat approached them, frowning, and Ella addressed him with fraught urgency. "She's impaired," she said, perhaps the least comprehensible descriptor to offer a man who had thus far only addressed her in Spanish, but Ella didn't want to insult him with dumbed-down English and, reflexively, didn't want to insult Jill, who couldn't understand anyway. "She doesn't understand," Ella clarified apologetically, still pulling on Jill's flailing arm. It seemed he understood, and he helped Ella, berating her with an anger that seemed almost tender, in words she couldn't interpret.

They went back to the pond after that, and then to the truck, which Jill still wouldn't get in, and then circled the lot like boxers, sizing each other up. It was humiliating, having to physically intimidate a shrieking disabled woman in public, but Ella succeeded in her most pressing goal, which was to keep Jill away from the construction site. Had Bryn been inside for hours? It certainly felt like it when, at last, he emerged, pushing the bike along with a triumphant smile on his face. He squeezed Jill's shoulder affectionately, and once the bike was loaded, they climbed into the truck's cab. He was eager to tell Ella the ins and outs of his adventures in bike repair, how he had been on the verge of giving up when he'd found the only part in the entire shop that would work, and what he'd had to do to prep the bike, and to attach the pedal, but Ella only half listened, trying to decide what to say when he was through.

Normally she wouldn't want to tell an employer about a near disaster on the job, but she never wanted to find herself in another situation like this one, and she felt it was important that he was made to understand the difference between how Jill interacted with him versus her. She couldn't control her like he could, couldn't guide her, could offer only so much bumbling, unwelcome protection. She kept it brief, tried not to sound like she was complaining.

He nodded in assent, and then went back to talking about the bike. He took pleasure in his success, it seemed—was that what this was about? Was he pleased to have demonstrated some competence? Was this a welcome departure from the drift of his days, where nothing, it seemed, had a tidy, practical solution? Was it an affirmation of his manhood? Or was Ella only looking for ways to feel better about accepting his help? When, at the end of the day, he handed over her crisp twenties as usual, she refused them with color creeping into her face. "You shouldn't pay me for helping me," she said, and, with a hardness to his face, he put the money back into his billfold.

She left with an uncertain feeling, like perhaps what she'd done wasn't right, but equally sure she would have felt worse accepting the money. What had that hardness been, that coolness that had crept into his gaze? And why had she really refused the money? If she were honest, she had been thinking of Nick, picturing him embarrassing his dad over it, criticizing Ella for taking advantage: "First you pay her to read the paper, now you pay her for the privilege of fixing her bike? Jesus," he would say, as if Bryn were a silly old man, helpless in facing the manipulative wiles of a sly young woman. She couldn't bear it; she had been determined to prevent it. What had made it unbearable? The truth in it, of course, for it wasn't Nick saying these things but Ella's own head. Not the bit about Bryn being a silly old man but the sly part, the manipulative part, for why had the rightness of Bryn's solution struck her? Because she was a girl who didn't know how to fix bikes, because he was a man from a generation that saw this as reason enough to do it for her. It wasn't the chivalry that had appealed to her but the convenience of it. **At last,** she'd sighed to herself, **a bit of the patriarchy working in my favor,** disregarding, for the moment, how inconvenient it was to live in a culture that discouraged mechanical aptitude in women.

Only that wasn't Bryn's fault. It wasn't a tidy equation where this was the tax on his privilege; it didn't work like that, especially since it could never come out even. It wasn't fair to either of them to pretend it could, for Ella to simper and blush and accept it as her due, for Bryn to stretch manfully, roll up his sleeves, make things right. Was this also part of the subtext for Bryn? Part of his chilled response to her squinting, pedestrian weighing and totaling? Perhaps he'd thought they'd struck a different kind of bargain, one where her wide eyes had said, "Daddy, please?" to which he'd sighed with a muscular largesse that said, "Okay, sweetheart," except that in the end, instead of the implicitly promised demure gratitude that would remind him he was a man, she'd put on her spectacles, taken out her checkbook, and queried, all business, "What do I owe you, sir?"

Maybe she had made him feel foolish, having offered to pay her for the favor he had done, as if he thought she was a princess, as if an opportunity to be of service was its own reward. Or, so much worse, maybe it had been an act of gratitude, this help he had offered her, and she had refused to be thanked, had refused the intimacy of owing him as, perhaps, he felt he owed her. **He doesn't owe me any thanks,** she thought, a little unhappily. She didn't do nearly enough for him, and the idea of his gratitude embarrassed her, that the meager, compensated tasks she performed might stir a disproportionate tide of feeling. It showed the vastness of his need, how it weighed impossibly against the heartbreaking modesty of what he expected from her, and again, unwillingly, she confronted the wince in his stride. The irony, of course, was that she had earned the refused wages today like no other; it had been the hardest shift she had ever worked with Jill. It felt petty to even consider that angle, Ella thought, a little wretchedly, as she pedaled home with remarkable ease.

· 12 ·

"I leave town Wednesday, want to get a drink tonight?" Liz asked.

"I'm getting a drink with Liz," Ella yelled down the hall with her phone twisted away from her mouth.

"Have fun. Tell her hi." Alix was in the depths of a project and couldn't be bothered to glance up, even when reaching for a plate of food.

Liz had been Ella's first girlfriend, when Ella was nineteen, a college freshman. Liz was now finishing up her PhD on the East Coast and they didn't see each other often, but when they did, Ella felt like a version of herself that she didn't otherwise seem to have access to. It was like spending a prolonged chunk of time with her mother; she reverted into some earlier incarnation.

As she walked through the door of the neighborhood bar, she saw Liz standing, talking to two strangers, holding a beer that was already half empty, wearing a baseball cap crammed over her short hair. Every bit of it was so very **Liz** that Ella paused and took a preemptive draft of nostalgia that blended affection with irritation, for Liz's extroversion had always wearied Ella, and Ella could never even begin to keep pace with her drinking.

They embraced, and as Ella dragged her toward a booth, Liz wrapped up her conversation with the strangers in friendly shouts. Within fifteen minutes Ella's irritation had bloomed into exasperation, and yet she decided to nurse that same first beer for the rest of their conversation because she was already having trouble not kissing Liz, not settling into those familiar arms. It was a good thing there was nowhere to dance here; Liz had always been a dangerously good dancer.

"How's Alix?" Liz asked early on, and when Ella replied, "Great," she saw that Liz was both disappointed they were still together and pleased Ella was still gay. She had always hated it when Ella dated men, and presumably it had little to do with wanting to date Ella herself, because the time when it had counted, that time when the breakup actually **took,** she had been the one who had ended it. Ella assumed the reason Liz would prefer her single now was so that they could fuck, and also, like others Ella had dated, because she would like to hold Ella in reserve, a backup plan for the long haul in case nothing more suitable came along.

They talked about Liz's thesis, and all of her numerous Plans, for Liz was a Visionary, she was practical, ambitious, and well girded with upper-middle-class money and self-assurance. Ella was confident Liz would end up famous, if only in lesbian-feminist circles, but were there more interesting circles to be famous in? Ella had her doubts. And then Liz wanted to know about Ella's plans, and this made Ella feel suddenly tired and sad. Liz already knew all about why Ella had dropped out of graduate school, she both understood and didn't—or, at least, if the **reasons** didn't mean much to her, she recognized the gulf in class background and temperament that made an advanced degree a means to an end for her and for Ella, an intolerable experiment in upward mobility. Ella's plans involved sitting with Jill for six hours the next day, posting an ad for a roommate for the time Alix would be in Spain, taking the Greyhound to visit her grandmother over the weekend. In contrast, Liz's plans involved, among many other things, founding an international nonprofit. Liz nudged Ella to set her sights a little higher, with an impatience that felt like love. "We need you," she said softly. "We need what you have to offer," and Ella was overwhelmed with a desire to cry.

When they said good-bye under the streetlight, they hugged exactly as long as they could without kissing, soft cheek to soft cheek, breathing in the familiar scent of each other, remembering it clinging to pillows and borrowed T-shirts, remembering how it felt to be nineteen and ecstatically happy and frightened and alive. Still, it was with contentment rather than regret that Ella slipped into bed next to Alix's sleeping form. She didn't want to be with Liz, with her alarming gregariousness, prone to inviting three or four others to join them on what was to be a romantic getaway, with her eagerness for the next round when everyone else's glass was still almost full, with her too-keen insights into Ella's laziness and self-absorption, a tendency that somehow made both of them look and feel bad. And Ella wouldn't want to be nineteen again, not truly. The only part she really missed was the feeling that it all lay ahead of her, that it all might come easier than she dared hope. That planning time of life had shuddered with fear and promise, when the things that Ella could and couldn't do were yet to be determined and her quirks hadn't yet calcified into neuroses.

The years between nineteen and twenty-nine had been full of disappointments. It had been a decade of ruling things out, of finding everything just as difficult as she'd feared and maybe even harder. She had thought that she'd at least have succeeded in leaving by now, that her world would feel fresh and expansive from the vantage point of an exotic metropolis, some cultural hub that was far elsewhere, but her apartment sat exactly six miles from the house she grew up in. She hoped rather than trusted that her thirties would be better; even if they weren't, she was happier now, in her restless, pensive way, than she had ever been before. She loved Alix. It was too dark to see it now, but she loved the drawing Alix had made that hung across from their bed, and she smiled in its direction. She liked that she could ride her bike to work in the morning, flying past the sugar maples that would soon be transformed into crimson aureoles. She liked that Bryn would greet her with real gladness, and that these days, Jill would periodically sit with her in front of the picture window and watch the wind tug the changing leaves, and then, when Jill rose to resume her self-imposed pacing duties, Ella could comfortingly regard the empty house about them like a clock, with Jill the ticking second hand and Bryn, upon his return, a scheduled chime, signaling it was time for tea, and in between, all the notched minutes and hours were marked by Ella's hands, holding book or charcoal or threaded needle and loose button, or scrawling dreamily over the pages of her journal while Jill folded towels or murmured to her baby doll. At such moments, she wasn't even sure what more to want, for the stillness so utterly suited her.

· 13 ·

Ella stubbornly biked to work in the rain even though taking the bus might have shortened her exposure. She was going to get wet either way, she reasoned, so she might as well save her bus fare. When Bryn opened the door for her, she was embarrassed about how wet she was, her pale face dripping and gleaming as if the rain had washed all the color out, her leggings soaked from the tops of her rubber boots up to the point where the bottom snap of her raincoat cinched it shut. This was not how a professional began her workday. She had grown too comfortable.

"Um, maybe you want to let me in through the garage?" she asked, but Bryn just shrugged and went to find her a towel as she eased her feet out of the boots, followed by the socks, which stayed behind. Ella very much wanted to remove her wet leggings but, though her shirt was longer than some dresses she wore, she couldn't imagine herself nonchalantly talking to Bryn without pants, her shirttails parting suggestively when she sat, her naked legs curled beneath her on the sofa. When he returned with the towel she dried her face, her hair, and then the length of her legs, as if the tight black fabric were actually her skin, and the practiced motions felt like a strange demonstration of what she did each day when she got out of the shower, only this time with clothes and an audience, although she noticed Bryn had politely averted his eyes.

Bryn's serious expression matched the prediction she had formed when she'd first seen the sky through her bedroom window, for she now knew his moods and their triggers as well as she knew Alix's. It didn't occur to her that he might also know hers, in part because she felt like an observer inserted into his natural habitat, where she would always be the self-conscious outsider, and he would have the illusion that everything was the same with or without her presence, a lulling sense that he was in his private realm; also, because she tailored her moods for the demands of the job, smoothing her face and voice like a tablecloth, her irritation or tiredness or boredom showing only faintly, like residual fold lines crisscrossing the table's length. Still, after so many months, could he read her? Did he care to try? She never thought to wonder, for she was simply the help; she trusted that her moods didn't matter if she didn't subject anyone else to their ripples and sighs.

Ella decided she would put her leggings in the dryer when he left, wrapping a blanket, if she could find one, around her legs as a barrier against the chill air, but Bryn just stood and looked out the picture window with an expression that suggested the sky had betrayed him. "Let's have our tea early, maybe it'll clear up," he said, with more defeat than hope in his voice. Ella resigned herself to more time sitting wet, but the tea offered a cheering promise of warmth.

They settled into their usual places. Jill was coaxed with her usual plate of cookies, unaware that she wasn't supposed to be hungry for them for several hours yet. Cautiously, Ella tried to soften Bryn's frown, with partial success. They talked with what Ella considered a comforting normalcy, the easy informality of the everyday, the same chip in the plate as yesterday, but also the memory of yesterday's meal. Ella liked the way, more and more often, they could replace a word or even a laugh with a glance, or not even a glance, an assumption that the other understood, so regularly reinforced there was no need to seek proof. Served on the everyday dishes was the everyday stuff of life; they didn't venture into the abstract. Bryn told her about how he got the scar on his thumb—an occupational hazard of carpentry. They commiserated about relatives with regrettable political views and compared notes on their respective trips portaging in the Boundary Waters. Ella boasted about the fat northern she'd caught and eaten, and Bryn genially let her ride her victory. He wasn't the sort of man who needed to one-up, unless he was provoked, usually by Nick, who seemed to believe that any show of strength from his father was designed to prove he was still a child. There was ample room for affection, even respect, in their rivalry, though the strain of Jill's decline sometimes lured their less admirable traits to the surface.

Ella routinely made allowances for that, excusing minor lapses here and there, but somehow the cumulative effect didn't register, maybe because she wanted to believe that she **knew** Bryn, at least to the extent that she was able, for his inner life and his outer seemed sectioned off by temperament and also by long habit. She didn't acknowledge that, overall, she wasn't getting the best of him, or even the ordinary him, but the least favorable version, worse, even, than during the shocked, panicked aftermath of Jill's accident, for adrenaline provides strength, but the extended grind of Jill's descent left him powerless, diminished, with a thread of rage and an ache of grief. Why was this so hard for Ella to see? Because she still refused to examine his injury, as if it were skin torn off his shoulder in a raw patch the size of her hand, now bleeding, now crusting over unhealthily, now weeping fetid liquid. She believed if she looked at it squarely, her own shoulder would throb unbearably, that his suffering might be contagious, that there might not be any cure, that she would leave his house, return to her ordinary life, and suddenly find she could no longer lift the knowledge that Alix would one day die, that Ella would, too, her shoulder would strain against this once-manageable dread, mirroring the weeping of Bryn's wound.

Ella had just arrived and she and Bryn stood a few feet apart, with Jill busily brushing imaginary crumbs off the table into her hand. Bryn smiled, with a strange tightness to his face, and the usual spark in his eyes was glittery, almost hard.

"My mother died last night," he said.

"I'm so sorry!" Ella said, and she moved as though to touch his arm, and then hesitated, hovering, her head tilted up to meet his eyes.

"It's okay," he said, still smiling that strange smile. "The memorial will be on Tuesday in Denver. I'm going to drive, and I'm trying to decide if it's crazy to try to bring Jill. We've taken road trips in the relatively recent past, and she's fine in the truck for long periods of time. But what happens when she needs to go into a ladies' room without me?"

Ella knew he couldn't send Jill in alone. She tried to picture him bringing her into the men's room at a truck stop or a rural McDonald's and there was something profoundly humiliating and wrong about the image, far worse than a woman bringing a disabled husband or son into the ladies' room. It made her feel protective of both of them. She wanted to shield them bodily from the curious glances of imaginary cowboys at urinals. She wanted to take Jill to the ladies' room herself but knew it would be impossible.

Ella had heard of Bryn's mother, of course, that she had moved into a nursing home near where Bryn's sister had ended up, in Denver, and that she had been in her nineties, and that her health had been poor. She knew her name was Clara. She did not know if Bryn loved her or missed her. She did not know if Jill had gotten on well with her mother-in-law, or if Clara had been a comfort after the accident, if she had been capable of offering meaningful support in her eighties, or at any time in her life, for that matter, but then, Ella had never asked.

When Ella did ask Bryn questions, they were about the work he'd done before he retired or about his childhood. She rarely asked about Jill, and when she did, she again felt like a daughter whose mother had died before she was old enough to know her, as if she was stepping into this complicated mourning that was more absence than loss, or, rather, loss experienced as Bryn's, as opposed to her own. When he answered her gentle questions, she would respond shyly, as though invited into a tender place, even though their language was unemotional and Bryn's tone suggested that his grieving lay far in the past. Ella knew it wasn't so. His grief was there, in his tense jaw, in the cords of his weathered throat, in the knuckles of his rough hands, in the corners of his mouth and the furrow of his brow, in his laugh. The strength it must have taken to contain that suffering, so that only the edges showed, so that a stranger's glance wouldn't exactly read them but might snag on something ambiguously raw in his bearing or his voice, it amazed Ella. It also put her in the peculiar position of being able to let the whisper of it fall into the background when she didn't have the energy for empathy.

Later, at home, Ella felt pleased that she hadn't overstepped her role, hadn't tried to draw him out, make him talk to her about things that weren't any of her business. Why would he want to tell her? Who was she to him? Just a girl who came over so he could leave to buy groceries. She was pleased she didn't have to be embarrassed now, didn't have to cringe in blushing regret, remembering how he had flinched away from her attempts at comfort. Except she wasn't glad, not really. Relieved, but not glad, because maybe this kind of regret was worse, not regret that she had been her usual bumbling self, trying to force things that couldn't be forced, but regret that she

hadn't tried, hadn't risked minor awkward-
ness out of kindness. He could hardly ask
her for comfort, even if he were the sort
of person who would; it was, presumably,
outside of the scope of her job description.
She should have hugged him, whether he'd
wanted her to or not, because that's what
you do when your friend's mother dies.

If she had, she suspected, he would have
been stiff, uncomfortable with her touch.
They never touched each other; they never
even sat next to each other on the love seat
or the sofa. This seemed almost chivalrous
on Bryn's part, like he was always aware, in
a generational sense as much as anything,
that they were a man and a woman, and he
didn't want to make Ella uncomfortable.
Even when they were both standing in the
den, the space seemed too small, Ella would
feel eager to tuck herself out of the way,
into a chair or a corner. Bryn was tall, it
was true, but it was more than the scale of
him. His presence took up space, and he
seemed to require a buffer zone, although
not with Jill, he was affectionate with her

in an easy, friendly way, scratching her back as you might that of a puppy, holding her hand, kissing the top of her head.

Ella also felt disinclined to touch Bryn. It would be like being thirteen and hugging her friend's dad, it would maybe give her a weird feeling, the unavoidable contact of her breasts with his body, him tense with the fear of being misread as lewd. This was actually how Ella thought of Bryn, sort of, like a friend's nice dad, one she might chat with when fetching a glass of water from the kitchen; he would ask how school was, how her mom was doing, and if he was driving her home and the friend couldn't come, the conversation would be easy. He would always be perfectly appropriate, and Ella would get that weird feeling only if she didn't put a bra on right away in the morning after a slumber party. Not that he would look, but there would be a prickly sort of shame in the room with them, if her nipples were poking through her tank top, if her full but adolescently pert breasts moved when she walked past him. They were both infinitely happier if they weren't forced to recognize her nubility, and the specter of maybe not **his** susceptibility but that of older men in general. Ella tried never to let that specter into the room with them, so perhaps that was why the den felt too small, from a mutual fear that proximity might be misread as intent. **Misread** being the key word, for it felt improbable that Bryn would actually be attracted to her, since Ella imagined his type to be more mature, certainly, but also fit and outdoorsy. It was not improbable because Bryn's virility didn't seem in any way compromised by age and disappointment. That would have felt far safer. His masculinity was as much a part of his presence as the quiet hum of his sadness; Ella could hear, or maybe feel, the twin currents, even when her back was turned to him, both tugging at her, softly, disconcertingly.

· 15 ·

After a year of creative spurts and lulls, Ella had finally finished a painting. She knew it was done because she couldn't think of anything else to do to it. She had worked from a photograph she had taken several years earlier of her grandfather and a friend, small figures walking away from the observer into a gray winter afternoon. Her grandfather was by that time already well into the shuffling of Alzheimer's, and as crude as Ella's painted figures were, she believed you could see the affliction in the awkward stoop of his posture, his coat too large and his hat obscuring his face and head from the back, so that he contrasted with his friend, who stepped tall and graceful beside him, white-haired, his indistinct face turned toward the smaller figure.

"It's done," she called to Alix, and she listened for the sounds of Alix putting clean dishes away to stop. Alix, a blue checked dish towel still in her hand, walked over to the sunny corner of the bedroom where Ella's easel faced the window. Alix looked at the painting, and Ella looked at Alix looking at the painting. "I love it!" Alix exclaimed, and Ella exhaled a bit. Alix would compliment almost anything anyone wore to make friendly conversation, she would compliment mediocre cooking and forgettable decor, but she never lavished praise on art she disliked. Art mattered too much to her for pretense, and her feelings about what made art good were too intrinsic to her being to allow her to misdirect people. It would violate her integrity, although she wasn't likely to articulate this in such a way. It was simply a kind of sacrilege for her to praise work that she found false or pretentious or lazy.

"It isn't very skillful," Ella said. "I'm not very good at figurative rendering. You can tell from the figures that I don't draw that well."

"I think the naïveté is core to the poignancy and sincerity of the work," Alix replied. "There's a sweetness that isn't cloying or manipulative. There's love for your grandpa in the lines of his form, there's love of birches and pines and snow in the lines and curves of the landscape he moves through. It's wonderful."

They stood quietly and looked at it together for a long moment.

"You really need to paint more," Alix said, and they both knew what she meant: it seemed like Ella might be able to do it well, but they would never find out if she didn't put in the time. A frequently neglected painting every one to three years was the path of a hobbyist, with hobbyish results. Ella was still satisfied with the painting, though, because while it fell short of her artistic vision, it had successfully translated her emotional vision into something tangible.

This seemed especially significant because virtually everything Ella owned was secondhand, had originally been chosen by somebody else. It was never the pitcher or afghan she would have chosen out of all pitchers or afghans; they were merely quirky gifts the thrift gods had left for Ella to find. They worked for her because they were lovely, they were well made, they were carefully combined, they had taken many hours of searching, they had cost very little money, but Ella had never set out with a **specific** vision of what her ideal afghan would be; likely, at the time, she wasn't even searching for an afghan—she had just walked into Goodwill looking at every item for something beautiful.

That sort of aesthetic was almost the opposite of custom-made, while her painting was the **definition** of custom-made, it was made up of the images and the colors and the composition chosen by **her** out of infinite options, hindered only by lack of skill and the limits of her imagination.

Bryn and Jill were back from the funeral, and Bryn had said little about it. Ella was quietly concerned about him and had been pleased when he'd said that he would frame her painting for her, she had asked if they could do it in barter for her hours, and he had agreed readily enough. She had thought about this for a little bit, and then said she would, of course, pay for the supplies, and also that it shouldn't be an even exchange, because his work was so much more skilled and taxing than what she did with Jill. "It **should** be an even exchange" was all he said, and that was that.

When Alix drove her to work with the painting, it sat in the back with the image turned toward the seat because Ella imagined it was safer that way, although from what she couldn't say. She removed it from the car and carried it across the street with the image also turned toward her body, and when Bryn opened the door to let her in she hesitated briefly on the threshold. "Well, here it is!" she said, and, recognizing it was unavoidable, she flipped the canvas to reveal her work. Bryn's gaze didn't linger long on the painting, but Ella scrutinized his expression nonetheless. There wasn't any discernible trace of softening or smiling in his dark eyes, there was nothing in the hold of his mouth or lines of his forehead to suggest appraisal or contemplation. There wasn't even a polite muster of moderate enthusiasm, a searching for something, anything to admire, as one might for the enthusiastic but meaningless scribbling of a small child. Finally he commented on how big the canvas was.

This didn't bother Ella much, not just because she knew the painting wasn't great but also because not much in his house was to her taste. She liked the furniture he had made because he had made it, because it was beautiful wood pieced together with tremendous precision, because she liked to picture him in happier times, absorbed in the task of creating, but most of it had a Zen quality that didn't speak to her. The one piece she loved was damaged: a pretty credenza missing a chunk of one exquisitely crafted sliding door. She grieved a little for that missing bit of wood each time it snagged her eye.

Ella had thought Bryn would buy some simple pine boards, cut them into thin strips, stain and attach. Done. Instead, he told her he'd dug through some treasure trove of wood scraps, she didn't know where—were they from his own old woodshop?—and found just the right length of birch. It looked like valuable wood, but Bryn wouldn't put a price on it, wouldn't let her pay for it. He had to take it in his truck somewhere with commercial-grade machinery to split and cut it and miter the corners, which he somehow managed to accomplish even though, as he had gravely informed her, the canvas wasn't properly squared. (She had apologized shamefacedly for her inexpert stretching.) Each step was explained to Ella over the course of several shifts, until the day she came and found Bryn set up in the yard oiling the gorgeous, naked wood in a patch of sun. Nick was there that day doing laundry again, and he and Ella stood and watched his dad work through the picture window. Bryn had told Ella that it was requiring several applications, but that it was really letting the beauty of the wood show through. She wondered, a little uneasily, if Nick had watched him do this with each coat, repeatedly walking out to the makeshift table, stooping to coax a sheen into the wood with the friction of his hands. It seemed suddenly like far more than she deserved, she felt embarrassed to see it through Nick's eyes.

Why did Bryn's dedication to the project discomfit her? She had hoped he would enjoy it, enjoy the chance to make something pleasingly solid. She had tried, again and again over the months, to encourage him to pursue some sort of hobby, to join a support group, consult a grief counselor, get a gym membership, build something, read something, see a movie, go for a hike or a bike ride, anything to get him out of the house and, ideally, out of his head. It was true that he puttered in the garden, but the growing season was short in Minnesota. There was the Community Ed class he had been so enthusiastic about during the interview, although in reality it had taken months for him to work up to even looking at the registration forms. Now he was doing something, and with pleasure, just as she had hoped. So she was the lucky beneficiary of his effort; why should she feel defensive? Perhaps because her painting wasn't really good enough to warrant such loving craftsmanship.

"Is that my mom and dad?" Nick asked, glancing at the painting where it leaned against the wall. She supposed it **could** be Bryn and Jill, the tall, white-haired man guiding the shorter, hunched figure; still, it seemed a little presumptuous somehow, as though the hours she spent working there weren't enough, and her creative work must also be consumed by them. "Oh, no," she said with a smile, to soften the denial. "It looks like it could be them," he offered, a friendly observation. Perhaps it was his way of including Jill in this creative collaboration that was more truly about Ella's private painting, Bryn's patient labor; a friendship that Jill sat in the center of without actually being able to join in.

When the frame was finished and the painting snugly inserted, the effect was terrific. The frame had the austere beauty of a Shaker chair or bureau, perfectly complete in its simplicity, the natural wood grain gorgeously emphasized through the oiling. It was the ideal aesthetic for the scene it contained, the wintry trees echoed in the coolness of the unvarnished blond wood. Even the depth and thickness of the frame filled Ella with a wonderful sense of inevitability. Only this frame could so utterly belong to this painting, it was custom-fit, not only in its dimensions, which corrected the slight warp of the stretcher, but in the sensitivity of all its particulars. Even if Bryn didn't care for her painting, he had succeeded in making it entirely more successful.

They looked at it together, Bryn quietly gratified and Ella effusive. Would Bryn like to do more for barter? Ella had only one or two more paintings that were maybe worth framing, though there might be more in the future. No, he would rather not. Ella tried not to sound disappointed in her response—she had only hoped he would **want** to, she didn't wish to pressure him. She had hoped this would be a solution for both of them: for her, beautiful frames; for him, something to do and a way to save money during his time away from Jill. She felt, a little sickeningly, that it had been more work than he'd anticipated and less pleasurable than she'd allowed herself to believe. She stopped there, with her guilt and disappointment, reluctant to ask herself why he might have done more than he had the energy for, or why it had seemed to give him pleasure.

Bryn drove her home that night with her painting carefully wrapped and secured. As they made their way through the darkening streets in silence, Jill unhappily squished between them, Ella thought, still chewing her uneasiness, **Probably he did all of that work because he said he would, that's the kind of man he is. Probably he did such an unnecessarily artful job because that's the kind of craftsman he is.** And then her thoughts slid to Alix, and what she might be making them for dinner.

When Ella carried the painting in, she placed it quietly on the sofa, image facing out, before joining Alix in the steaming kitchen. She thought, **I'll just leave it there until Alix sees it—no need to make the frame into a big deal.** But Ella frequently decided not to say anything and infrequently held to the decision.

"Well, Bryn finished the framing," she said while looking into the empty teak salad bowl that sat on the counter.

"Oh?" Alix said, closing the oven and pushing back her damp bangs.

"It's on the couch," Ella said, and followed Alix into the living room.

Alix looked at the frame, her expression unclear.

"It's nice. Though it's kind of old-fashioned, the way you think that art has to be **framed** and hung formally on a wall." She turned back toward the kitchen, saying, "Will you fix the salad?"

Jill sat on a chair in the yard surrounded by autumn leaves, slack but not entirely passive. Bryn and Ella stood, combs and scissors in hand, and strategized inexpertly about where, and how, to start cutting. Bryn rested one hand reassuringly on Jill's shoulder and spritzed her dense bangs with a spray bottle. She recoiled, complaining inarticulately, though offered only minimal resistance. Ella pulled the comb through the ragged mass and snipped timidly as dull clumps of hair tumbled free. These days Jill's hair always seemed to look like a dirty wig, something one might wear to play the part of a homeless person. These periodic efforts to shape it prevented Jill's vision from being obscured but did little to help her appearance. The lack of skill applied combined with the constant movement would have rendered their efforts farcical if the results didn't matter, but somehow, to Ella, they did.

Of course, Jill was well beyond caring; she didn't even recognize herself in a mirror, and would have long, nonsensical conversations with her reflection. Bryn treated the haircut like a practical matter, like making a meal or vacuuming, something to check off his list. Ella didn't like for Jill to look crazy, or dirty, or like her clothes were for a larger woman, because it compounded her vulnerability, or at least highlighted it, made it visible to strangers on the rare occasions when they all went into public. It wasn't that Jill's decline was shameful; it just felt somehow private—not like a secret but like something sensitive to shield from curious eyes. Ella wanted Jill's every encounter to be respectful, and the choppy, almost waxy hair combined with her shuffling and mumbling didn't invite respect so much as prompt discomfort, avoidance, averted gazes, crossing the street.

Ella was aware of Bryn's body, so near her own, so different from the four- or five-foot distance they both usually seemed to need to feel comfortable. She had thought she'd known his face and frame as well as she knew the rooms of his house: the brown of his eyes, so dark they were almost black, and the jut of his cheekbones, and the set of his shoulders, all of him observed day after day like the ever-present bananas dangling from their hook over the buffet, and the wedding invitation that was always on the fridge door, and the faint smell of the compost bucket in the sunny mudroom off the kitchen. Now, so near their hands occasionally brushed, it felt rather like she were opening the buffet drawers to find details to his physicality that were normally obscured by distance, lines, and stubble. Even his hands, on which her eyes had rested thousands of times as they'd talked, seemed new to her, rougher, larger.

She took in his brown wrists, shirtsleeves

pushed up over his forearms, such a contrast with Jill's unpredictable hands and dirty nails; the small gleaming scissors; the tendrils of hair floating down to the grass. It was so strange to actually feel the heat coming off his body; this somehow made him feel more **real** than he ever had before, like seeing a television personality in the flesh. She noticed his hair needed cutting, too; it was falling over the collar of his shirt, and she briefly considered offering to trim it as they released Jill from her chair. Would that be overly familiar? Immediately she knew it would be; she reared back from the thought, a little disconcerted, and followed Jill inside, leaving Bryn shaking out the hair-covered towel Jill had worn around her neck.

They had tea, as usual. Ella was making her way back from the bathroom when she was surprised by the sound of the doorbell, and then a little panicked to hear Alix's voice carrying down the hall: "Hi, I'm here to pick up Ella if you're through with her."

Ella rounded the corner into the living room and found Bryn standing next to Alix, who had known better than to introduce herself, but Ella felt she couldn't let this get any further out of hand.

"Finally you meet!" she said, with forced cheer. "Bryn, this is my partner, Alix." He looked very surprised, then quickly regained his composure.

"So nice to meet you," he said, shaking Alix's hand. Ella's embarrassment about the situation mingled with pride: Alix was so very beautiful, standing there with her mass of golden hair, her enormous brown eyes, her endlessly long, slender legs. She felt bad that it mattered to her how Alix looked, how men envied Ella, the surprise that registered when people saw they were a couple, as rare as unicorns, the mythical feminine lesbians, hands entwined.

She tried to get a read on Bryn's response—was he hurt that she hadn't told him before she'd been forced to? It seemed unavoidably so, but likely he didn't want to seem as though he were justifying her hesitation by acting less than delighted. They left quickly, with shy smiles. When they got to the car, Alix said, "Sorry about that!" And then, "You didn't mention he's so handsome."

· 17 ·

Ella and Alix lay beside each other in bed, looking up at the lazy rotations of the ceiling fan.

"Well, he knows now," Ella said.

"It can't really matter, can it?" Alix asked, taking Ella's hand and squeezing it too tightly, as she often did.

"Probably not to Bryn, at least not beyond the weirdness of me not telling him sooner," Ella said.

"Do you feel relieved?"

Ella paused to consider this. She did feel relieved in one sense, certainly, albeit with an edge of something vaguely unpleasant.

"Yes, though I also feel, not embarrassed, but maybe a little ashamed? Not of being queer but of revealing myself as a sexual being or something. I don't know—it's confusing."

"I never really understood all this sex-shame stuff," Alix said, turning onto her side to look at Ella.

"That's because your parents are atheists."

"If you could do your childhood over, would you grow up without religion?"

"If I could do my childhood over, I'd change a lot of things."

"You would still want to have gone to church?"

"It isn't really about that, about church." Whenever Ella tried to make sense of her religious upbringing, she quickly gave up; it was such a mixture of comforting familiarity and pain. And it felt so unchic—not the remnants of her faith but her confusion—in contrast to the seeming flexibility and simplicity of Alix's moral worldview.

"What were the good parts about it?"

Ella paused before answering, and they

could hear the footsteps of their upstairs neighbors overhead.

"I guess the importance of awe at something larger than oneself. Only it's costly, because you recognize your own smallness. And it isn't just awe—I can feel awe at a mountain or a thunderstorm. It's awe at something both inside and outside of, of **me**," Ella said. She lay quiet for a bit, considering this, and then she realized Alix's hand was slack in her own. She'd fallen asleep.

Ella could remember exactly where she'd been, exactly what she was doing when God died. Not when Jesus died on the cross but when her heavens emptied—when she became, for the first time in her life, alone. It had been soon after graduating from college, an ordinary night without a precipitating event. She'd been lying in her grandparents' guestroom and enjoying the summer moonlight and she'd thought, **Well, what if it isn't true?** She'd thought it idly, with an almost cheeky curiosity.

Only even just thinking it was like the time, as a child, she'd been curious about what would happen if she stuck something in the electric outlet. It almost threw her to the floor, the entire structure of her world collapsed on top of her, she remained dazed and shattered for hours. For a time she pretended nothing had changed, but that didn't work. Eventually she thought, defiantly, **Well, I can** choose **to believe in God if I want to.** Nevertheless, choosing was a far cry from knowing, it was like choosing to believe you'd win the lottery, rather than knowing you would inherit a fortune, although with stakes inexpressibly higher. Not because she had hoped for an afterlife—heaven had never been a big selling point for Ella—but because of life itself. Everything was difficult and bleak enough even **with** the comforts of faith, **with** an infinitely loving and omnipotent force overseeing it all. The loss had been nearly unbearable. She had sought an example to follow in her grandfather, in the clear blue of his eyes, honest and free yet lonely, the terrifying beauty of godless heavens, only her internal experience differed from what she observed in him. She had felt more broken, unmendably broken, than free. She no longer had access to redemption.

Ella still grappled with that same sense of brokenness, of self-loathing. It seemed impossible that she might love herself. Then recently, just walking down the street, she'd thought—unbidden, almost a revelation— that she needn't love herself, that the task could be God's. She was beloved if only she could believe in the lover. For a moment she'd felt such relief, that the burden of loving herself had been lifted, she'd felt as though the impossible were no longer being asked of her. Her world, however, no longer fit tidily into that equation as it once had. Ella was untroubled by picking and choosing the bits of Scripture that suited her; it wasn't that. It wasn't that she'd come to see religion as a crutch for the weak, for she was admittedly weak and saw no crime in crutches anyway. It was that some part of her rebelled at the thought of reembracing, so unquestioningly, the sinfulness of her nature. There was poison in her, but was she poisonous? Was her essence poison? Was there nothing large in her that was her own? Sometimes the holy in her felt as real as her conception of God. She was practiced at self-scrutiny, she knew how to bow her head in repentance, yet while she was no stranger to willfulness and pride, she believed she knew nothing of the posture of majesty. Was there room for humility in the Divine? This question wasn't abstract for Ella. This question had made her cry, walking down Hennepin Avenue.

More troubling than these questions of divinity and redemption was the devastating solitude. In the days after losing God she would lie alone in her bed at night with just her restless limbs, just her cascading thoughts. Before the dark hadn't sat empty above her, and the corners of her room, though shadowed, had been warmed because they were inhabited. Perhaps a different sort of human would have known how to fill the darkness. Such a person would have heard the wind in the trees outside the windows and thought of all the years of growth, all the nights of breezes, all the trees in the world and the trees that stood before and were gone and the trees not yet planted. There would have been thoughts of all the people sleeping in the surrounding houses, and all the people who weren't sleeping, and the world would have felt, maybe, full. Even though now she could still summon these perceptions, they couldn't make her feel. What she'd used to feel had been more than a feeling; it had been a knowing that her consciousness never sat alone in a wooden chair in an empty room, never watched the light coming in through the window slant longer and longer, never watched the light fade, never listened as darkness fell in silence. It had been knowing that her consciousness never ceased to be in conversation. Could the never redeemed like Alix fathom what any of that meant? To trust, from one's earliest knowledge, that one's every thought was heard and considered? Censored, yes, but she'd never claimed it was without cost.

It had become easier to bear the solitude once she'd met Alix. The solitude had remained a part of her, inside, though companionship was such a comfort. She reached and stroked Alix's slightly sweaty hair—Alix had night sweats nearly always, like a napping toddler—and she ran her index finger down Alix's cheek. Alix surfaced just enough to squeeze the hand in which hers still rested but didn't open her eyes. Ella reached inside herself, seeking the bit of loneliness that was ever-present. In this moment it felt indistinct, and Ella was grateful.

What was her spiritual practice now? She thought of Bryn and Jill, of the fullness that knowing them gave her. This wasn't the job she'd planned on; she'd planned to join the creative class, she'd planned for upward mobility, she'd planned to wear lipstick to work and to earn a salary and to earn it with her mind, but there was something wrong with her, something wrong with her mind, only her hands could be directed, assigned mental tasks evaded her, slippery-sieved, and this was the job she had now. Still, wasn't there beauty in the practice of love and the roll and sweep of it? This question carried her past her late-night wakefulness. She rolled over, pulling Alix's arm around her waist, and they nestled together in the darkness.

· 18 ·

The bathroom was filthy, absolutely
filthy. Everything seemed to smell like
decay, like Jill's unhealthy saliva and sus-
piciously unclean hands. No doubt there
were traces of feces everywhere: on the
ragged towels that were strewn throughout
the rooms, on the dingy pillowcases that
had worked their way off the limp pillows,
on Jill's pilled fleece hoodie with stains at
the wrists and down the front, on the worn
slippers she would slide off and on, again
and again. The battered sofa. The throw
blanket Bryn's sister had crocheted that
neither Bryn nor Jill had ever liked.

Now winter was emerging, the wind
sliced, the yard no longer invited. They

would be captives in that drafty house until spring, shuffling, raw-knuckled, from chilly room to chilly room, dragging tattered bathrobe ties behind them. Shoveling icy steps in early darkness. Hibernating in the bleak glow of the television set. Bryn and Jill had always been creatures of summer, of warm nights, cold drinks, the outdoors. It seemed to baffle Bryn to observe Ella's enthusiasm for fall, and now winter. Ella loved the coziness, and even the chill. She loved the moodiness, the landscape bleached of color, the guilt-free hours spent curled up indoors with a book, a drawing, a new recipe. Before too long it would be Christmas.

Bryn was out on the front porch, and Ella imagined him observing the dreary sky. Perhaps he was wondering if the season's first snowfall would come tonight. Ella imagined he felt largely indifferent. The wind was terribly cold, and likely he hunched into himself, flicking ashes from his cigarette over the railing. Maybe he was picturing Ella and Jill inside, the baby gate latched to contain them in the den, Jill like a bumper car, bouncing from surface to surface, irritable, unfocused, Ella with her legs curled under herself, reading a novel, clutching a mug of tea. She imagined Bryn thinking of her, thinking that Ella could wrest tranquility where others couldn't, and that Bryn suspected this was a learned art, something that came from years of tedious, distressing caregiving work. One took the rewards that were available, he might think, given the circumstances. Whatever made things bearable.

Ella counted the pages left in the essay she was reading, as though this, and not the time, indicated how soon her duties would end. It was like reading to stop being hungry. It never worked; the words sped or dragged by and the hunger remained, words were not food, but there was this illusion of industriousness, as though goals beyond enrichment or entertainment might be achieved.

Ella sighed and pinched the book shut,

glanced at Jill through the doorway to the bathroom, where she was, once again, running the water in the sink, her hands frigidly cold and wet, splashing senselessly, patting her face, muttering. Ella had herself on a schedule so she wouldn't go insane, turning the tap off over and over. She would turn it off only every five minutes, if Jill walked even a few steps away from the sink. Ella was the sort of person who turned the water off while she brushed her teeth, used a basin of soapy water to wash dishes. Mindful of waste, perhaps even a little compulsive, and it all felt so useless, watching Jill—what was the point? What happened when Ella wasn't here? Did Bryn spend all of his hours turning the tap off? Did he wake regularly through the night to check the sink? It was maddening to consider. Ella wanted to shut the water to this sink off, by closing the valve itself, but Bryn's weary apathy seeped into her, and Ella understood, because what would Jill do with the water off? Reach into the toilet, even drink from it. And closing the bathroom door would just mean that Jill couldn't use the toilet. There were no tidy solutions.

Bryn came home a few hours later minus evidence of how he had spent his time away, his chapped hands dangling empty from the sleeves of his worn jacket. His nose was pink, and his eyes were dull under his shaggy hair. Ella pictured him walking around Lake of the Isles, a lonely figure in the cutting wind, but she didn't ask where he'd actually been. Bryn held his hands over the clanking radiator to warm them, and Ella looked around guiltily, thinking she ought to have done some tidying up in his absence. Bryn never asked her to clean, and this made Ella very happy.

The fact that Bryn never expected her to clean made her feel guilty for not trying to make Bryn's life easier. If she really cared, wouldn't she scrub that bathroom? She asked herself this, again and again, but she couldn't bring herself to do anything about it. Every time she sat to pee and noted the scent of stale urine, the grime and

balls of dust and hair accumulated on
the floor, she felt a surge of motivation.
She would scour this bathroom; it would
be an act of tenderness. And then she
would return to the couch and a collection
of short stories, or a volume of poems, or
her own journal. She would either pretend
she would clean the bathroom later, or she
would try to push the possibility from her
mind, almost like pretending there was no
bathroom, and the guilt would encroach
on the edges of her pleasure in the book,
sharpening it even as it became tainted.

Bryn looked gaunt; his flannel shirt was
wrinkled, the collar twisted in the back, and
Ella wanted to fix it, as though this might
fix other things, a sort of domino effect of
care. Avoiding joining Ella on the love seat,
Bryn moved a pair of shoes Jill had stuffed
with a magazine and a hairbrush from the
easy chair to the floor and sat warily, as
though he distrusted comfort. Ella got up,
turned off the water, sat down. Moments
later it was on again, and Ella tried not to
wince. She checked to see if Bryn looked

annoyed, but he was beyond noticing such things.

"Did you get a chance to look at that website I sent you?" he asked.

"I did," she said, "but I found it a little overwhelming. I don't really know how to narrow it down, since I don't know your finances. I'm sorry." Bryn had finally admitted that it was time to look at care facilities and had asked Ella to help with the research, telling her to keep track of the hours spent. She had agreed reluctantly, only because she couldn't bear to refuse him; she was so bad at that kind of thing. There were reasons she wasn't a social worker.

"Are you coming over tomorrow?" he asked.

"I can," Ella said, "if you like."

"No, that's okay, I just couldn't remember," he said, and she felt a little relieved. It was silly, what would she do at home? Read but without getting paid an hourly rate to do so. But it was worth it, to enjoy reading without having to turn off the water every five minutes, without the nightmare that was changing Jill's clothes, made worse by the newly frigid house. Ella was always cold there now. Then she looked at Bryn, and pictured him alone with Jill all the empty hours of the day, and heard herself saying, "I'll come at three."

· 19 ·

Once, when Ella was sixteen, her high school study group had met at her friend Dai's house. Dai had spoken perfect, unaccented English, but Ella had known that his family still spoke Vietnamese at home, and as he led the study group up to his bedroom, Ella felt him watching her absorb the foreignness of his house, the unfamiliar food smells, the strange silence of the adults, and, especially, the un-American lack of clutter, the sparseness of the furnishings—not the minimalist sensibility of the wealthy but an austerity that seemed somehow embarrassing to observe. It wasn't exactly deprivation, it was like they didn't understand, or didn't have access to, the material indicators of middle-class America.

The students sat on the floor of Dai's immaculate bedroom, unfurling the familiar paraphernalia of textbooks and papers as if setting up a picnic. Everyone's self-consciousness had begun to dissipate, although Ella still felt as shocked by how orderly the room was as she might have been if it were unlivably filthy. Where were his **things**? She thought of her own room at home, with its dirty linoleum floor, and walls scarred with nail holes and ragged posters and cheap prints from the thrift store, almost every inch covered, framed greeting cards, her collection of dusty antique hats hanging on a crooked mug rack, pictures of Jesus, and the junk that filled every imaginable surface, psychedelic candles she never lit, and wrinkled scarves used as runners, and paperbacks crammed everywhere the eye might rest, and CDs, and abandoned dirty dishes, laundry, and homework assignments, and bottles of nail polish, and a space heater, because the room had no heat vent and the windows leaked so badly that an inch of ice would form on the **inside** in the winter, and she could melt her handprint into it if she could tolerate the biting cold.

She marveled at the emptiness of Dai's room, like a monastic cell, and carelessly tipped open the door of a shallow cupboard. Everyone stared in silence at the narrow shelves, perhaps four inches deep, and the symmetrically stacked bundles of white sport socks alongside tidy, meager squares of folded briefs. "Ella!" her friend Naomi scolded as, shamefacedly, Ella pushed the door shut.

Now, standing in Bryn and Jill's bedroom, she revisited that feeling of voyeuristic unease as she took in the absence of ornamentation, of any kind of comfort. The room had been stripped down to the necessities so that there would be less for Jill to get into while Bryn slept, but it was more than that. The down comforter had no cover; Ella imagined that, when Jill had been well, such details were seen to, and in this light it seemed like a symbol of Bryn's helplessness and defeat. The pillows were flat, the sheets smelled stale, the walls were almost bare, and Ella felt as though she were seeing Bryn naked. It was like walking in on him taking a shit, or masturbating, or weeping, something terribly intimate and solitary. Ella came here only when, like today, she needed to change Jill's clothes.

She leaned against the bed and tried to form a strategy. Jill was busy at the dresser, where she had discovered a glass of water. First she put her hand into it, as deeply as she could, so that water spilled over the edges, and then found a hairbrush to stir it with. These days Ella never knew whether to be slow and gentle or quick and efficient, to get it over with before Jill could work herself up into a storm of violence. Neither approach made things easy, and, like so much with Jill, it just seemed arbitrary, whether she was moderately or excruciatingly uncooperative. Ella said, "Jill, I'm going to help you change your clothes," and she felt a little like a hunter thanking a slaughtered animal for feeding her family, a ritual of respect, unheard in any literal sense by the violated.

Carefully, she removed Jill's reading glasses, which sat crookedly on her face and were so dirty they compromised her sight more than they aided it. Jill protested in her inarticulate way, but as soon as they were swept from view they were forgotten. Next, Ella contemplated Jill's soiled sweater with foreboding; it was such a battle to remove the garment that they did this only once or twice a week, as the food particles accumulated and the cuffs became dingy with whatever her eager hands reached into. Ella gripped the hem of the sweater and pulled it over her head as Jill screamed like she'd been stabbed, or like she had just received the news of the death of her child, a tortured sound, painfully loud, as loud as a person could keen, and she hunched protectively, clutching her thin undershirt, as Ella gripped it from behind and pulled it off, wincing at both the volume of the cries and also the suffering she was unwillingly inflicting, and Jill's small breasts hung slack on her wasted frame, the notches of her spine were visible, and her shoulder blades, and her mouth was twisted open in a howl as drool ran from the corners, but like a child who produces more noise than tears when throwing a symbolic tantrum, her eyes were largely dry. Now cold, Jill did not fight against the new undershirt and turtleneck, which was not the same thing as cooperating, for Ella still had to snake twitching, flaccid arms through tunnels of cloth, had to guide her head through the collar like a midwife with a crowning infant.

Next came the difficult part, and Ella winced in dreadful anticipation. As rapidly as she could, she unbuttoned Jill's pants, gripped the waist of her jeans, and yanked them to her ankles, while Jill pounded Ella's face and shoulders with both fists as if she were being sexually assaulted. And perhaps that was indeed what it felt like, which was a horrifying thought to Ella, but it would be no more of a kindness to leave her draped in filth, to let urine and feces encrust her, and it would be a terrible unkindness to leave this to Bryn, with whom Jill was equally resistant, and so, blocking the blows with one hand, Ella used the other to guide Jill into a sitting position on the towel she had draped over the edge of the bed, and then she pulled pants, slippers, and socks off in two calculated tugs, and Jill moaned and slapped and hollered, her saliva dripped to her skinny bare legs as Ella coaxed her resistant feet into jeans gathered into two pleated doughnuts, and she jerked them up until Jill buttoned them, reflexively, wanting to be covered. Ella pulled on clean socks and slippers with a mounting sense of relief, and then she sat beside Jill and stroked her back, then hugged her and told her she had done a good job, and Jill quieted like this was good news or, maybe, like she was entirely spent.

These encounters were unlike virtually anything Ella had experienced, at least in her adult life. Even the safest childhoods involve physical struggle, the battle of a will that doesn't know its own interests pitted against the almost divine strength of grown-up forces, capable of effortlessly pinching tiny feet together and lifting them skyward to shove a cold wet wipe between diarrhea-smeared buttocks. Adulthood like Ella's—which is to say, removed from poverty and war, minus prison or domestic violence or sexual assault— involved a kind of physical freedom that was easy to take for granted. Nobody touched her with anything resembling unwelcome force; violence remained, happily, an abstraction; and her physical space felt, if not so cherished as to be sacred, at least secure. No adult had ever struck her before Jill. It was physically jarring, the stinging fist against her cheekbone, her ear throbbing painfully, her own shirt torn askew, but worse were the internal repercussions.

It felt strange and awful to overpower a vulnerable person, to cause another person fear. If Ella was slow and tentative, as she sometimes was, especially in the early days, ten minutes of unpleasantness would stretch instead into thirty minutes of chasing Jill around the bedroom as if she were prey, Jill screaming with such deafening ceaselessness that Ella became convinced the neighbors would call the cops. She left no gentle approach untried before mostly settling on speed and efficiency. She never hurt Jill, never so much as spoke sharply to her (she was not a naughty child, capable of learning a lesson); Ella received her blows and scratches with passive determination, for her hands were seldom free to block a fist, to protect her face or eyes. Still, she felt like a malevolent bully, like a sadistic prison guard, though she experienced no anger, or pleasure, in thwarting Jill's will.

Beyond this struggle, she further had to contend with the unavoidable violation of Jill's privacy, a result of Ella's uninvited gaze. Ella's familiarity with Jill's body was unsettling in part because she didn't like to imagine anyone gaining such dispassionate knowledge of her own. Who besides herself knew, or cared, that one foot's arch was higher than the other? That a freckle sat companionably next to her belly button? Ella imagined that Jill had looked at, say, the contours of her own small hands a million times in the decades before her accident, had memorized the shapes of her fingernails, the rosettes that formed the knuckles of her thumbs. All of this remained except for the once-freighted familiarity of these traits, the memories of her child hand holding dripping fruit or her father's shirttail, her adult hand grasping that of her lover or the steering wheel on the day of the accident. Now it was Ella who knew Jill's body, but only in this stark context of helpless anxiety, of wincing under the hot pins of the showerhead, of eternally bracing for injury that couldn't be anticipated or precluded.

· 20 ·

D o you think she has another UTI?" Ella asked Bryn, and they both glanced over to Jill, who was sitting on the toilet crying with the bathroom door wide open.

"I guess I'd better bring her back to the doctor," he said. They were so often matter-of-fact about these things that Ella could sometimes pretend that Bryn could summon the same state of detachment she did. This pretense permitted Ella to say things that might otherwise feel impossible, like "She's definitely getting worse" and "We should plan now for when she will eventually have to move" and, calmly, "It's amazing how well she is able to articulate her sense of loss and isolation." All true, though not things you could say to someone visibly broken, unless their endless brokenness wearied you, started to break you, until you were hoarse, rough, blunt with fatigue and grief. Bryn shrouded his brokenness in quiet. It wasn't for Ella's sake, it was just who Bryn was, how he coped with the impossible, but it benefited Ella just the same.

Later, when Ella thought of her frank appraisals of Jill's condition, sometimes she couldn't believe herself, that she had spoken to Bryn as if he were just Jill's nurse, as though they could both regard moving Jill to a facility as simply the next necessary step rather than the next impossibly painful thing that must somehow be endured. And, in that light, Bryn's stoicism didn't make things easier, because then Ella had to live with the knowledge that she had been tactless, whereas with a cue, she might have been gentle, might have been able to look back at her words with the soft glow of assurance that she had done her job well. Ella felt bad about this for a while, and then it occurred to her that maybe, when one daily confronted the Abyss, the fragility of everything one loved, the permanence of loss, pussyfooting around difficult truths was not desirable. Maybe there was no place for coy euphemisms at the front lines. Maybe a blunt appraisal suggested that, truly, they faced this together, that Ella was looking at the Abyss squarely, too, and she had Bryn's back.

Bryn essentially lived in hell, Ella knew this even if she didn't always acknowledge it. It was like he was confined to an empty white cell with nothing to do but observe the sights and sounds of the torture of the person he most loved. Jill was able—surprisingly, painfully able—to communicate her loss of self, her impenetrable solitude. She would chant a mantra of loss, "Crazy, crazy, crazy, crazy. I'm a nobody. I'm a nobody. I'm a nobody. I have nothing. I have nothing. I have nothing. And I'm a nobody. I'm a nobody. Say say say say say. Stay with me! Stay!" And then the weeping, mouth wide open, drool and tears, hunched and clenched tight in helplessness. And then the rage, the poisonous incoherence. The meals eaten like a toddler, or an animal, furtive, desperate, or uninterested, or pizza dropped in the water glass, the water poured on the plate. The endless messes, also like a child, except one who doesn't learn, who does the opposite of learning, one who forgets how to use the toilet rather than becoming toilet-trained, one who will fight having their clothes changed as though their life depends upon it, only with the strength of an adult, screaming as though assaulted, naked terror on her face, hitting, kicking, slapping, scratching.

In certain moments, Ella felt an intense desire to enter into Bryn's grief truly, not to sample it like an emotional voyeur, not to pretend she could be heroic and save him, but to offer his suffering a united front. But then she would suspect that maybe, truly, she was just a child who knew nothing about real loss, who playacted at expertise she only knew how to mimic, who naïvely refused to understand that observing suffering gave one merely a vicarious sort of knowledge—flat, misleading, even dangerous. Maybe her advice was smug, maybe it wasn't really necessary, only gave her an opportunity to feel important, to pretend that this work both bequeathed and required some sort of skill, some sort of hard-won insight, that it wasn't just glorified babysitting, washing soiled sheets, microwaving some leftovers, passing a glass of apple juice to whichever client so that they might swallow the baby aspirin, and the Coumadin, and the statins and the Celexa, lisinopril and metformin and Sinemet and the Aricept and the stool softeners and nitroglycerin, as necessary.

Maybe it wasn't about Ella at all. Maybe Jill and Bryn stood on this pinnacle of grief, and the decades of their shared lives spooled out behind them, and then the delicate, fading years before they met, adolescence, childhood, infancy. Maybe they stood in this tenuous, haunted place and looked out upon the vastness of their lives, their accrued wisdom, their pooled joys and disappointments and triumphs, and Ella was outside of all of this, observing from behind glass as she pushed the vacuum in haphazard lines around their coffee table, behind their sofa. Maybe all of living was taking place somewhere else, somewhere Ella wasn't, in a skyscraper in New York, in a gallery in London, even in memories of places she had never seen and, it seemed, never would.

Sometimes Ella tried to imagine what Bryn thought about her. The temptation, of course, was to imagine flattering doses of gratitude, but she didn't fully permit herself that pleasure, not without tempering it. She imagined that the first thing Bryn liked about her, before they really became acquainted, was the way she threw herself into loving Jill with a reckless determination, as though there were this one thing she knew how to do well and she would do it with messy exuberance, like a stout little girl clutching her new brother a little too tightly, kissing his crumpled face resolutely: you are **my** brother, and while I can't know you, screaming wet ball that you are at this moment, I **will** love you. I will sing to you and talk to you as if you understand, and pour you tea you won't drink, and tuck blankets about you that you don't want, and wipe food from your face, which will make you turn your head angrily, but it is an act of love, because to see you wet or dirty, to imagine you hungry or scared, it is unbearable to me, it makes me fierce, and I **will** put that sock back on your bare foot, fight all you like, but it will be done, because it's cold, and how else can I show you I love you? She imagined that this touched Bryn in a way competent professionalism wouldn't, this inept fumbling for a grip on the beloved, the total absorption in the task at hand, as though it mattered to Jill, and who was to say it didn't? Perhaps in Jill's unreachable place, she could feel the warmth even if she couldn't understand the words.

Yet it couldn't go on endlessly, this arrangement, even if Bryn's endurance were infinite, which, Ella guessed, he must increasingly suspect it wasn't. Ella thought his fatigue must have begun to feel like a part of himself, like a physical disability that could always be counted on to complicate the tasks of daily living. But Jill was getting worse. Ella figured that at this point she probably almost never slept through the night, which would mean that Bryn remained near the surface of sleep all through the dark hours and into the haze of dawn, on edge, tensed, now dreaming, now listening, now dreaming, until morning, or until Jill got up, muttering, pacing, splashing in the toilet, removing books from the shelves to destroy, laughing mirthlessly, her reading glasses crooked and smeared, her breath like death. And the evidence that any of her circumstances influenced her quality of life was increasingly scarce; it was undeniable now that living with Bryn, in the house they had bought together—sharing meals, sharing their bed (although, for many years now, just for sleep)—mattered only to Bryn. Jill would mutter or shuffle just the same somewhere else, would weep and grieve somewhere else, would clutch an inanimate object like a baby somewhere else, would, perhaps, hold another hand as willingly as Ella's or even Bryn's.

An outsider might think that there was relief to be found in these thoughts, that the rewards were so scant and the demands so intense that Bryn might even be yearning, in a distraught way, for this next step. Ella knew, or at least believed, that was not the case. All that Bryn had left of Jill was her physical presence and her need. When she was no longer present and no longer needed Bryn, she would be gone. It would perhaps be like the day of the accident, Bryn's terror that he would lose her, Bryn's relief that she had survived, now, fifteen years later, reawakened only to be extinguished. It was like planning Jill's death, it was like pulling the plug, the guilt was unfathomable.

· 21 ·

Bryn left the house quickly now when Ella arrived, the slight of this offset by how reluctantly he released Ella at the end of her shift. Ella had some sense of how harrowing the hours before her return must be because her own time with Jill had become increasingly painful. It wasn't that the work had become much harder. She was still mostly sitting, mostly turning off the sink, battling to change soiled clothes or trim grotesque toenails, trying to prevent the destruction of stray objects—paperbacks, tubes of lotion, even table lamps, the laptop computer. But it was as if the frequency at which Jill's despair hummed had been sped up, the atmosphere of the house charged with a frenzied anguish.

Ella tried to draw Jill in her sketchbook, only it was like trying to draw a creek in the springtime: engorged, furious with the rush of melting ice. It was as if Jill were on speed, and when she crashed, her weariness seemed more complete for how meaningless, how endless her tasks had been. How does one decide when broken reading glasses have been adequately swirled in a drinking glass? When a foot has been slid in and out of a worn slipper a suitable number of times? Is four sufficient? Is twenty? What bearing does the presence or absence of a threadbare sock have on this magic number? Is now the right time to remove the sofa cushions? How about now? Is now the right time to empty all of the electrical sockets? How about now? If you'll excuse me, I must turn the water on in the sink. I've been meaning to wash this magazine all morning. I've been meaning to open the toilet lid. To close it. To open it. To close it. I've been meaning to sit on the toilet,

straining and crying with the door open, failing to shit, and then, succeeding beyond our
wildest dreams, a stool as girthy as an arm.
How does one work this flushing mechanism?
No matter. Are you thinking what I'm thinking? That's right. It's time to fill this box with
towels. Not all of the towels. Never all of
the towels. We must leave room for the shoes.
One shoe. Two? One. **Say say say. Saaay.**
Saaay. I'm a nobody. I'm a nobody. I have
nothing. I have nothing. I have nothing.
Saaay. Crazy! Crazy! Saaay.

Still, Ella managed to read, to scrawl
in her journal, even, at times, to join Jill in
her crying. It was a task they could share,
this attempt at relief. It wasn't that Ella
was usually so close to the edge. It wasn't
like she made a habit of crying at work.
It was more like it felt appropriate, even
companionable. If Jill had been her friend
in the more usual sense and Ella came to
visit, if Jill were grieving a stunning loss,
they might sit, hand in hand, and weep.
Ella had no other comfort to offer, at least
initially, to this person who was beyond the

reach of language. Just touch, and tears, and the abstraction that was Energy, in which Ella almost, barely believed. Her perspective on such matters was shaped by two seemingly incongruous forces: on the one hand, the rote skepticism of a college-educated, midwestern humanist; on the other, a conversance with **unseen forces** rooted in her evangelical upbringing. Both shared a discomfort with anything relating to magic, touchy-feely hippies, life force, etc.

And yet, Ella carried with her, quietly, almost shamefully, certain moments that were burned into her memory, of a mysterious touch that carried more than the heat of its parts; not sexual but strangely powerful. Ella didn't know what to call it other than a transfer of Energy, and even that was only to herself. She didn't talk about it with anyone else, afraid of sounding foolish or, worse, like a self-important, pseudo-spiritual yuppie.

The first instance was the last time she had visited her grandmother's closest friend, a beautiful, tiny old woman who'd perched, sharp-eyed and sharp-tongued, in her wheelchair, with a spare but radiant smile that combined the caustic power of her remarkable mind with warmth, so loving without being **sweet**. Ella had no reason to believe it would be their last visit, and yet her love for Ruth overwhelmed her, made her feel a sadness that was almost desperate. As the two families mingled and chatted with the ease of very old friends, Ella felt compelled to stand behind Ruth, silently, with her hands resting on the older woman's shoulders. She was tentative—they were none of them an overly affectionate bunch—and yet, delicately, her fingers met the rough cardigan, and the gnarled shoulders beneath it. Abruptly, it had been like her hands were singing, or like her young blood flowed through her fingertips and coursed through Ruth's veins, through the chambers of Ruth's heart, through her all but useless legs and weakening organs. It was almost impossible not to weep; it took nearly all of Ella's strength to ensure her tears only flooded her eyes without tumbling, tellingly, down her face.

Months later, after Ruth's funeral, her daughter told Ella that Ruth had described that afternoon in her diary. She had written that Ella had a **healing touch**. What did this mean? Ella didn't know, but it felt right that Ruth had perceived the power that had transfixed Ella behind her wheelchair. When Ella's first client, Betty, had nearly died, Ella had gone to sit with her as she slept, almost unresponsive, in hospice for weeks before making a gradual recovery. She had placed her hand upon Betty's arm, this time with deliberation, and summoned the flood of love and power and tears. It had sprung, just as she'd beckoned, through her touch, it had flowed as if through a tap, her hand had grown terribly hot, and she had sat there, very still but for the crying, for as long as she'd deemed necessary.

Now, with Jill, this was all Ella could offer, and hours, broken into snatched moments, were devoted to its practice over the months. It was an exercise in futility, or faith, which amounted to the same thing, for hadn't Ruth died? And Betty, too, a few years down the road? If Jill could still conceptualize an abstract desire, beyond the animalistic cravings of hunger and exhaustion, it was, undoubtedly, to die. The strength of her body thwarted her; the eviscerated pulp of her mind all but screamed to be released from that fine-boned face, the freckled skin taut over the bridge of her pointed nose, stretching to form a corporeal cage of her delicate shoulder blades, ribs and hips, elbows, and toes; crowned, like barbed wire, by a tangle of reddish curls, still untouched by gray, floating above her slightly protruding ears.

Ella wove a spell of her own disparate mystical threads, the magical power of the Energy, the strange humility characteristic of prayer, with its distinctive blend of resignation and fierce, almost defiant hope, and a third component that was unmistakably **her**: the cool gaze of the humanist, who, in failing to prevent her from praying, at least succeeded in reining in the **scope** of her supplication. She didn't beseech her Higher Power to heal Jill, but rather, to comfort her, to bring her peace, to enable her to feel loved. Ella had no reason to believe any of this affected Jill, no tendril of promise escaped the bundle of stress and fatigue, but Ella felt only **good** could come of this meditation on love, even if only Ella could experience its glow.

And yet, a part of her mistrusted this meager, private comfort—indeed, all comforts. This was not, as one might think, the rational humanist dismissing pie in the sky but the ecclesiastic ascetic reminding Ella, in a solemn though self-abasing tone, that she had no power of her own, that Ella's every impulse led her away from Painful Truth, from Scouring Righteousness. In seeking to take comfort into her own hands, she shirked the inevitability that was death, the frailty of human flesh and will, the scourge that was suffering. The ascetic didn't believe that Jill deserved to suffer but held that Ella did, that there was a redemptive quality to facing this darkness without the anesthetizing tonic of her alleged **healing touch**, which, after all, only distracted Ella, leaving Jill to face her demons alone.

Jill's loneliness was a horror to Ella, it seemed the very worst in the bouquet of suffering and loss brain damage carried. It was this horror, combined with her own powerlessness, that provoked Ella to explore nearly every conceivable route to connection. The passing of Energy was one route, gazing steely-eyed into the darkness was another, weeping was one, or merely standing shoulder to shoulder and taking in the sunset, or the night sky, or the rain streaming down the picture window. Language, of course, was the most obvious, and seemingly the most futile, route to human connection. This did not stop Ella from trying, verbal creature that she was.

In the early days, there had been the pretend conversations, and when those had faltered, Ella had concentrated her words into the most spare and potent fragments, like poetry without metaphor, blunt, repetitive, almost musical: **You are loved. You are loved. You are loved. We are here with you. We are here with you. We are here with you. It will be okay. It will be okay. It will be okay.** This felt like pure, embarrassing foolishness, like the silly nothings a mother whispers to the warm, sweet head of her sleeping baby, and Ella never let Bryn overhear it. Where was Ella's rational self in such moments? She was beyond cataloging her anger or her sadness, beyond strategy or analysis. She was beyond self-consciousness, outside the seductive passageways of her capable mind. Ultimately, it was perhaps only in this state that she and Jill could occupy the same isolating plane of being: that is, feeling minus the perpetual buzz of thought.

Ella knew immediately that something was different today, even if only incrementally. Bryn leaned heavily against the windowsill and Ella stood where she could see into the bathroom, where Jill was noisily splashing and babbling at the mirror. Bryn said, "They can take her in three weeks."

"Three weeks?" Ella was shocked. So soon? It was past due but also abrupt. To her credit, Ella thought first about what this would mean for Bryn: the relief, the guilt, the newly empty hours to fill. And then she thought about what it would mean for her, to no longer come to this now so familiar house, to no longer speak with Bryn with the casual intimacy of people who see each other nearly every day, to, perhaps, never see Bryn again. And then she thought about what it would mean to no longer see Jill, and it felt like planning Jill's funeral. She would be sorry not to see Bryn anymore, but she would grieve Jill's transition like a death.

It was always so strange, the ending of these positions. The homes she worked in became like extensions of her own home, in some ways almost more familiar, for in her own apartment, she seldom sat and stared around herself for hours at a time. Her eyes would slide over the familiar furnishings and objects until each seemed almost like a worry stone worn smooth from fondling: the same table with white rings from sweating glasses, the same Indian corn in the ceramic bowl threaded with lacy cracks, the same ugly throw blanket, the same framed print and worn love seat. She had memorized it all, although not with any intentionality. She had her favorite mug, glazed blue, and she knew the one odd spoon in the drawer, and even the differences in the half dozen dish towels in rotation. She knew the quirks of the old vacuum, how the compartment where the bag went in would pop open and stop the suction, how the ancient attachments snapped into place. She knew where to find the salt to refill the shaker, and the brands of everything Bryn bought: which mayonnaise, which tea, which beer. She knew the patterns of wear in the runner rug on the stairs and the smells of all the rooms in the house—cool, old, slightly vegetal—and which windows stuck on broken sashes, and which light switches controlled which lights, and where the Band-Aids and spare toilet paper rolls were kept. She had spent so many afternoons contemplating the dust motes floating like gold flakes in a paperweight, drifting in the sunbeam that came through the den window as Jill drowsed, the house silent except for the hum of the refrigerator. It seemed strange that she wouldn't watch the season change in the yard again, from winter to spring, and then the lazy heat of summer, the string beans dangling on the vine, the heft of ripe tomatoes. It would all go from utterly **normal** to absent, and all of this acquired knowledge would become obsolete. It would never matter again, it would be time to start over with someone new, someone whose descent was already beginning, but just barely.

Ella hated the beginning more than anything; it was far worse than the end. The end was wrenching but finite: by that point Ella was indispensable, and usually beloved, like a member of the family. In the beginning she had to prove her worth, had to woo with her every ounce of strength, beaming with pleasure at each opportunity to be useful, mindful of every potential misstep, lulling someone who mistrusted a stranger in their home into believing they weren't sacrificing their independence through her presence. She had never failed to charm, people-pleaser that she was. They would love her within a month, she would be like a daughter, like a best friend, like a therapist, like an escort. The toll it took wore her down, each courtship felt like the last she could possibly endure. And yet, she never failed to love her clients in return, although sometimes their families were harder to like. Not Bryn, obviously.

She looked at Bryn now, barely able to contemplate what this would mean for their friendship. She wanted to ask for reassurance: Could she still stop in for tea? But it seemed so desperately beside the point, so utterly self-centered. The loss would be Jill, not Ella. She wanted to embrace him, but the thought made her so bodily self-conscious, she felt clumsy, overbearing, like a mama bear or like a stout madam with a customer, all bosom and squeeze. Instead, she went to turn off the sink Jill had temporarily abandoned.

Ella tried to imagine what Bryn must be thinking. Likely he had never felt so tired or so tense, like a bottle of oil and vinegar, half dread, half longing for this to be done. He must be forcing himself to consider all of the things that needed doing. The TB test. The transfer of prescriptions. The deposit.

Meetings and paperwork and more meetings. Perhaps he hoped Ella would be willing to stay for longer hours, just for this final push. It must seem unthinkable to do all of this alone. It probably seemed unthinkable that he would live in this house alone. He wasn't fool enough to try to sell it in the dead of winter. He could rent out the spare bedrooms to help pay for the heat, help pay for Jill's care. Bryn would have to be practical about that, as exhausting as it sounded. Likely he craved solitude for his grieving, or at least, he might think he would. Not for weeping, not for listlessness, but to avoid having to be polite, to avoid playing the role of someone who wasn't broken. Ella thought he wouldn't like showing a stranger which cupboards in the kitchen would be theirs, or sitting at the big kitchen table exchanging niceties over canned soup. Perhaps he could rent out the whole house, get an apartment. But then he would need to empty it, with the ice thick on the steps and sidewalk, without a yard sale, or furniture and a FREE sign at the curb. Spring would come soon enough for all of that. Ella might be able to help, although then again, she might not. She might be too busy with a new job— a strange thought to accompany so many other changes. He would miss her, she knew this, but that was likely more than he could contemplate right now.

Ella watched Bryn pull on his jacket and walk out the kitchen door, onto the back steps. The snow was packed down hard where the door swung out; he was probably aware he should have shoveled it when it was fresh, before this could happen. She imagined there were many things he had let slide in the last few months. The list of things that had once felt nonnegotiable probably shrank all the time; he hadn't planted any bulbs before the ground froze, he didn't plan meals for the week and carefully select the ingredients as he once had, and last week the garbage hadn't made it to the curb. She pictured him lighting a cigarette with numbing fingers and making his way to the truck. Bryn was heading to the nursing home, for that's what it was, really, you could call it a **care facility**, or a **residence**, or a **memory care unit**—it all still amounted to the same thing. There would be the smell of urine, the cries of the confused and angry, the depressing visual cues of decline: walkers with tennis balls on the feet, hospital gowns, medical-industrial cups in shades of dusty rose and baby blue, oxygen tanks, wheelchair-bound people with swollen feet sleeping in hallways, televisions turned up far too loud.

Most likely, Bryn could scarcely believe that this was what it had come to. He must know, truly, that it would make no difference to Jill, that Jill was well beyond knowing where she was, or who soaped her flailing body, what food she put into her mouth—that wasn't the distressing part. The horrible part, the thing that had almost certainly made Bryn wait this long, beyond what was actually endurable, was the thought of visiting Jill there. It wasn't as if they could talk to each other, Jill might as well be in a coma, for all the communication that was possible—in fact, that might be easier, for then Bryn could hold her hand, or sit beside her and read. Now Jill was all frantic energy with no useful way to expend it. Would Bryn come and watch her pace? Watch her move the meager personal belongings of whatever unlucky people shared her room? Watch her stagger about, crying, or talking nonsense to her reflection in the mirror? The answer was likely rarely, drifting, over the years, into seldom, and then maybe not at all, for Jill was still youngish and strong, and while Ella had never been told the specifics of either Jill's accident or her condition, it seemed she could live another twenty years, maybe more. It was so strange, how the end could precede death by years, by decades.

· 23 ·

Ella was asleep and then she wasn't. She had been dreaming about trying to make a pot roast, and then, suddenly, her waking mind intruded, thinking, **Did I pour out the water from Jill's footbath?** And, though the stakes were fairly low, her heart pounded, and her eyes fluttered open. Now that she was awake, the specific anxiety about remembering to tidy up seeped into a general anxiousness that filled every available crevice, like a toilet overflowing to cover the floor. These abrupt nighttime panics were becoming routine, even on her days off, when her ordinary life bubbled mercifully to the surface and she was able to focus on the bits of herself that were separate from her working life: how fun it would be to visit Alix in Spain that summer, how much she would miss her when she was gone, the party she would be attending Saturday night and what she would wear. The vague shapes of her next painting were beginning to come into focus in her mind, and while she hadn't so much as sketched it out on paper yet, visiting the idea of it, coaxing it into view, became a coveted place for her mind to rest, or maybe **engage** was a better word, for rest was too easily interrupted now; it took engagement to keep worries about Jill and Bryn at bay.

Bryn was utterly falling apart. Even his physical body was breaking down: his limbs were covered in a scaly red rash that Ella and Nick took turns pleading with him to see a doctor about. Ella suspected that he never slept at all these days. His constant irritability was like a thin crust protecting something unbearably raw, and Ella couldn't avoid testing his patience now and again with her tentative prodding—"I know you don't think a doctor will be able to tell you anything useful, but we could at least hear what they have to say. Maybe they could give you something for the itching" or "They'll just sedate her in the care facility anyway, if she were on a sedative now, maybe you could get some sleep" or "That's frustrating, but I'm sure Nick's doing the best he can." Bryn would stand at the picture window and talk without looking at Ella, clawing at his inflamed arms, so swollen his shirt cuffs wouldn't button. Ella could feel his misery diffusing in vapors that coated every surface of the room—the battered down vest he wore, the stained love seat piled with Jill's discarded towels, the shelves and desk and steps, Ella's hands and face and hair, the ceiling above them, the large pane of glass he wouldn't turn away from. His body was rigid with strain, and she noticed that his hair was slightly thinner than when they had met.

Ella thought, **No one touches Bryn but Jill.** The thought was sad and hungry and tense, like the hunched muscles in his shoulders. There was nothing she could do about it, of course. Bryn could barely stand to be in contact with his own skin, and even Ella's increased proximity in passing made them both duck and veer as if she were carrying a steaming pot of water to the kitchen sink. If at times she felt her physical presence was intrusive, at other times she felt as insubstantial as in the type of dream where one is merely an observer, disembodied eyes floating in the stairwell, watching Bryn manifest his defeat, watching Jill shriek and sob from beneath a crazed snarl of dirty hair. Of course, even her gaze felt intrusive, all the more so because she felt so impotent. This was truly what her nighttime panic was about: not whether she had left some menial task undone, but that she was failing—daily—to ease any part of Bryn's burden.

· 24 ·

Ella felt as though she had entered a war zone. Bryn stood in his place at the window, his posture stiff and tortured, his face almost gray with fatigue. Ella realized he had not met her eyes once since she had arrived. The tension in the room was shimmering and syrupy; Ella found it hard to breathe, and her heart rate refused to slow. This was made worse by the fact that she couldn't pinpoint the specific threat making her adrenaline surge and therefore couldn't talk herself down. She stood beside Bryn, within reach but without touching. They contemplated the old snow in the yard, the deepening shadows of late afternoon, the sky heavy, almost oppressive. Dead vines blew in the garden, and the wind cut in around the edges of the glass to bite them. As Bryn turned to look at her, Ella feared that his eyes would be dead. Instead, she saw that he was drowning, not in tears but in a kind of panic that was very still. Jill splashed in the sink behind them, but they were scarcely aware of it. Ella felt, abruptly, like she was on the verge of drowning with him, as though his grief were flooding the room, reaching her ankles, beginning to climb her calves. Jill left the bathroom and Ella fled into it, locked the door behind herself. She turned off the water and sat on the closed toilet lid. She was afraid she would cry, she wanted to vomit, there was so little of her armor left.

Ella thought of how, many months before, Bryn had described trying to take Jill to the Alzheimer's center for adult day care, how he couldn't bear for her to see the name of an affliction so much like her own written in a sign above the door, couldn't bear for her to hear it there, again and again, said so casually, for at that time she knew what it meant, knew that in some sense it applied to her. How many thousands of times worse must this be now? Ella bit her hand and tried to think what she should do. She would go back into the den and pull him to her; there was nothing else to be done. And then Ella's fear flared up between her and the bathroom door and she cowered. Would his sadness fill her? Would he push her away in discomfort? And then the worst of her fears overwhelmed her. How could she hold him without crying? Without her attempt to comfort slipping over the line that protected them both?

Somehow, she couldn't imagine offering him only a part of herself, she couldn't imagine real solace that ended after only a moment. She tried to imagine her hand, chaste and kind, upon his shoulder, only the image wouldn't stay within her control, his hands, scaly and inflamed, wouldn't continue to dangle or clench, but pulled her body and her psyche to mesh harshly with his own. The imagined scene played out in her mind, and Ella felt ashamed at the dread and yearning that washed over her. What kind of sickness was this, that his brokenness glimmered with erotic power?

It wasn't just that she wished to comfort Bryn. She felt aware of his hunger in a way that viscerally bypassed her thinking and emotional selves, it was like an inky-hot injection spreading through her veins and intestines, pooling fiery and viscous between her abdomen and the tip of her tailbone. His desperation stirred something wild and distasteful in her, she could almost feel the weight of him pressing her to the floor, her knees spread wide, her skirt bunched at her waist. She could almost hear his zipper and his breath, suddenly loud with his face pressed close to her own, with Jill whispering and pacing unseeingly at the periphery, like a ghost who manifests as chill where there ought be no draft.

She tried to shift her thoughts elsewhere, flung her attention to the dirty floor, to the dripping faucet, but still the specters loomed with sexual menace. She was sweating. A part of her, usually feared, usually shackled and ignored, longed to remove all barriers between herself and Bryn, to join him in the thrilling, sickening free fall of his grief. It would be like drowning beneath the ice lid of a frozen lake, or like kissing with a mouth full of broken teeth and blood. It would mean an exquisite, excruciating oneness. The door remained closed, though even out of sight she could taste the ache of his need. She felt lascivious and dreadful, tears burned in her eyes even as she succumbed to the image of his hands on her body, the pull of which she was abruptly forced to acknowledge. It was so powerful as to feel nearly inevitable, as though all of the days and months leading up to today had been discreet exit points Ella had stubbornly, incorrectly regarded as unnecessary.

He seemed nearly unrecognizable, her kind and rueful friend with the sadness just beneath his easy grin. She had always felt so safe with him. That wasn't true, or it was and it wasn't. He was safe in that he was so principled, so measured and restrained, so utterly careful in his dealings with Ella. The unsafe part was Ella herself, how, the moment they had met in that sunny, bare living room, there had been a certain warmth, a natural sympathy, which would have been lovely to encounter if he had been a plump and permed woman of advancing years or a grandfatherly fellow with chicken legs emerging from his shorts hitched high over a jovial belly. In either of those circumstances Ella would have thought, **Oh, I will like this job,** and that would have been the end of that.

Ella had read an article recently, an unserious snippet of pop psychology claiming that people register almost on sight, animalistically, whether each new person falls into the category of someone they would have sex with or not. This had felt so true, when Ella had read it, and involuntarily she had thought of meeting Bryn, of that quiet spark of recognition that had flashed within her. It had been the same last week at Alix's art opening, Ella had walked in and seen a woman so deliciously androgynous, so handsome and chic, that Ella had automatically smiled at her with frank admiration. The woman, standing next to what turned out to be her partner, had returned the smile, her eyes revealing the satisfaction of being admired by someone one admires in turn. Sexual compatibility had quietly flared between them, a pleasant charge that wasn't disruptive but likely followed each of them home that evening.

Ella didn't really know how Bryn felt about her, whether the attraction was mutual, and it was almost irrelevant. They existed on an island; there was no one else, only Ella, only Jill, only Nick and Lisa. There was no one age-appropriate and beautiful, divorced or widowed, offering chaste comfort aloud while silently planning her future with this Good Man who would eventually, tragically, become available. Ella had imagined this suitable girlfriend before. She would have a sleek, expensive haircut, the sort that professional women of a certain age could easily afford, and she would like biking and camping and a glass of wine with dinner. She would seem so patient when Bryn explained that he wasn't ready, and she would say, We can both use a friend right now, and he would accept that, and within three years they would be married. It had surprised Ella when she had imagined this, the twist of jealousy and dislike that had stirred in her. She resented this woman she had imagined, with her jutting collarbones and gym-toned upper arms and her muted desperation that Bryn would remain naïvely oblivious to. When Alix had picked her up that night, Ella had said, "Bryn will find someone else, don't you think? He's a catch for a man his age, even if he isn't working. A woman meeting him now, she would have proof that he would be a caring companion for old age. And he's so good-looking." Alix had murmured her agreement without enthusiasm, accompanied by a sideways glance that wasn't entirely pleased.

It had made Ella feel a little abashed, that glance. Hadn't they objectively acknowledged that he was an attractive man? He wasn't an acquired taste, it didn't take a discerning eye or quirky predilections to see his appeal. He was like Paul Newman or Robert Redford at sixty, the sort of man whose prime spanned three or four decades. Ella assumed that women, and yes, probably men, flirted with him at the grocery checkout, at the DMV and the corner coffee shop. Likely they had always done so and it hadn't changed as his hair had silvered and lines had etched around his penetrating, smiling eyes. Likely he took it for granted, the thoughtlessness of beauty in a straight man who is neither vain nor sexually opportunistic. His beauty seemed more remarkable with the seasoning of age, for aren't we all, to varying degrees, beautiful at the height of youth?

Ella felt guilty about her disparagement of Bryn's imaginary, age-appropriate future girlfriend. Why did the woman's veiled desperation inspire disdain? Why was it something she felt an urge to protect Bryn from? Why, in fact, did Ella imagine her to be desperate? She would be in her fifties, still younger than Bryn, but old enough that her singleness would feel abject, more permanent with each passing year. She would previously have grown increasingly resigned to some compromises. Maybe he didn't need to be taller than her. Maybe he didn't need a full head of hair. Maybe he could earn less than her. Maybe she would be smarter than him. And then Bryn would have appeared at her grief group, chivalrous, funny in his mild way, six foot three, with movie-star good looks. Decidedly earning less than her. Decidedly emotionally damaged. A fixer-upper, but such a desirable one. She could afford, at this point, to prop up his burdened eaves. That first day, she would have looked around the group furtively for competition embedded in its ranks. She would have forced herself not to swoop down on him as the session ended, would have forced herself not to metaphorically grip his wrist with her beautifully manicured hand.

This was absurd, and not a little sick.

There was no age-appropriate woman; every attribute Ella burdened her with came from within Ella's own internalizing of the culture's fear and cruelty regarding women of advancing age. She was a composite of Ella's insecurities, both about what she lacked now (toned athleticism; affluence; cosmetic and material polish; mature, bourgeois emotional restraint) and what she feared she might become (desperate in the face of waning sexual power; calculating; competitive; indiscriminate). Where did **indiscriminate** come into it? Because, although Ella admired and desired Bryn, although, in her way, she loved him, he was not the sort of partner she sought. Not just because he was old, and emotionally wrecked, and, well, her boss. Not just because he wasn't Alix, who was, after all, her actual, chosen partner. It was because he was too conventional, too male, too closed. Because, on the rare occasions when he irritated her, it struck her as in a particularly unsexy way. The transparency and predictability of his masculine rivalry with Nick. The grim yet manic smile that stretched unnaturally across his face when he was concealing something truer, darker, more private. The way she felt compelled, due to the intersecting motivators of people-pleasing and paycheck, to laugh at his less clever quips. None of it was his fault, not exactly, it was just that it reminded Ella that she was actually smarter, more clever, more verbally dexterous than the faux appreciation to which her relative powerlessness reduced her. It was her role, as girl and employee, to laugh, to burnish his tarnished masculine ego, to stroke it tenderly like a penis reluctant to swell. Yet didn't a part of her seek that role? Didn't that masculine vulnerability stir within her strangely maternal yet girlish longings, equal parts mother, daughter, and lover?

Would Bryn expect Ella to spend sleepy weekends playing with the grandkids? The idea was sobering. Not because Ella disliked children, she liked them fine, but because she had planned her life quite differently.

She never intended to give a single hour to any child's sporting event, it was a minor but cherished check in favor of the "no children" column. She loved Alix for a million reasons, and one of them was that there was never the ugly blare of sports-related broadcasts anywhere in their home. Another was the absence of masculine moodiness, the entitlement that permitted their sullenness to slosh onto other people's cheer. Likewise the absence of masculine neediness—Ella never suckled Alix like a baby. Really, men were so uninteresting, domestically if not sexually, but, often enough, sexually as well. Ella tried to remember whether she had ever enjoyed sex with a man, not measured by orgasm, something easy enough to achieve under all sorts of tedious or inhospitable conditions with a firm touch and a little grit. The better measure was whether he could make her want. Did Bryn make her want? The idea of Bryn made Ella want, but the idea was Ella's, her mind weighted by the heft of him, her pale limbs gripped in his coarse hands, his grizzled cheek hot against her face, or her thigh. It wasn't actually difficult to make Ella's mind want, it was trained along familiar, practiced lines. It guided each object of fantasy, whispering directions from offstage: You want her almost to the point of violence. You must be very discreet, risks abound. The wrongness of this is foremost in both your thoughts and hers. Had men made her want in the flesh? Women frequently had, women she had found only mildly appealing, only moderately interesting, could kiss her and she would feel something involuntarily shift and tighten within her, a small surge of heat that was mystifyingly visceral rather than cerebral, a shocking break from Ella's normal mode of being, living in her mind, her body a heavy, ignored vessel that moved her thoughts from place to place and occasionally distracted her with hunger, tiredness, and pain. Likely it happened with men, too, but unreliably. She remembered the disappointments more keenly than the rare and unexpected successes.

But it must be admitted that Bryn filled

her with a tenderness she didn't seek. That felt like the greater betrayal, as far as Alix was concerned: the way that tenderness was shot through with wanting, the way the tender wanting had grown even as it was starved, for Ella never fed it, never prodded or stroked it or whispered encouragingly to it in the moments before sleep. In all honesty, even the things about him that irritated her could be endearing, for love, as far as Ella was concerned, could not exist without the presence of imperfections. Not just because people couldn't exist without the presence of imperfections but because love wasn't two charmed vessels bumping rhythmically until they chimed, rang true. Love had everything to do with the ache of vulnerability. It was Ella's younger sister, crying, at twelve, with a stained sweatshirt and a crooked part in her hair, the tenderness splitting Ella wide open, unbearable. It was her grandmother overcooking the peas and carrots, and Ella cross, because they weren't tender-crisp for Thanksgiving, and the crossness not really being about the soft and pale vegetables but about her grandmother no longer being bigger than Ella, and infinitely more capable, and showing Ella how things should be done. It was about being cross that her grandmother's vision was going, and cross that she got tired now, and couldn't time it so all the dishes were cooked and relatively warm in the same brief window where a quick benediction could bring their forks to mouths in unison. Ella didn't want to be the one who cared most about things turning out just so; she didn't want the spot on the silk tablecloth from India to tear at her, a reminder of how everything was becoming less perfect, devolving toward incoherence and loss. The spot on the tablecloth was Gemma's crooked part, was Jill's dirty fingernails, was Bryn's forced grin and unfunny joke, was Alix's future crow's-feet and tea-stained teeth. It was love as anticipation of loss, it was love as shared burden of pain and embarrassment. It was pain transformed into gratitude, for without the ache, a stained tablecloth was merely flawed, merely unlovely, but the ache was like a caress on her grandmother's wrinkled cheek, a comb straightening the crooked part. Slowly Ella rose and opened the bathroom door.

It was spring and it had been six weeks since Jill's move. Ella had a book she thought Bryn would like, and she e-mailed him, said she might bring it by sometime. He said that would be fine and he had a little something to give her, too. She didn't go. It just seemed like, once work with her new client, Nancy, was done for the day, it was easier to go home, or to get things for dinner, or take care of that phone call, whatever. Bryn was fine. Probably.

And then one day Ella felt uneasy and she tried to put her finger on what it was. Hadn't she done everything right? Hadn't she been professional? Hadn't she been sympathetic, supportive? A friend? Wasn't that what he had needed? And then it occurred to her she had done what was safe, which wasn't necessarily the same thing as what was loving. She had felt so proud that she had kept herself under such tight control, and now it seemed that it hadn't been anything nearly so admirable, for the veneer of will had been girded by fear. She had held him at arm's length, that was what she had done. She had determined he didn't want or need anything more from her without trying to find out if that was actually so. It was done, and Ella grieved. And then, she decided, she could still apologize, which was a terrifying thought, all of the risk without any of the reward, for his need was now gone.

And so, she found herself at his door, her stomach in knots. Ella expected him still to be grieving, but she also trusted that he had turned some kind of corner. When he opened the door, it was clear that this was both true and untrue. The tension was, if not gone, different. It felt like the ruins after a terrific storm, when it was still unclear what might be salvaged from the wreckage.

There was his face, his wonderful face, all of the smile lines that had once creased and warmed her days, there was the essence of him, so different from remembering the essence of him, she felt his presence in front of her and she also felt it inside her. It was different because he could see her and she could feel seen, feel recognized if not known. It was lovely and it was unsettling. Ella embraced him as she began to panic. She tried to talk herself down—she could still be vague. She could still leave things unsaid, resolve to visit more often in a friendly manner. She wasn't locked in.

They sat on the couch in the afternoon sunshine and spoke about how Jill was, and Ella's new job, and how Bryn was doing, although in no meaningful detail. Ella noted, almost bewildered, how little the room had changed. Even the sunbeam was the same sunbeam; even the lamps remained absent. Bryn thanked her for all she had done. Ella said, "I can't help feeling like I should have done more," which was something people say. People say they should have done more and often they mean that they wish what they'd **actually** done had **helped** more. Bryn had likely encountered this before, developed his own abrupt, blank-faced reassurances to use again and again, and he started to you-were-great her, to there's-nothing-to-regret her. Ella interrupted.

"I feel like I need to say this," she said, and he waited. Her hands were icy and damp, and her abdominal muscles were all tightened. She didn't know if Bryn was looking at her, because she was looking at her feet and at the window and at the room's single plant, glossily unchanged. And then she looked at him and he was looking at her but she could read nothing in his face except for stillness and the stillness seemed almost unreachable. Almost, but perhaps not completely.

"I think I did a, well, an **adequate** job as an employee," she said. "I did, most of the time, what I was asked. I failed on a few fronts, but we were still feeling out my role together. And I think I should have been more intuitive about what you reasonably needed but didn't ask for, especially once I figured out you weren't the sort of man who asks for more help easily." It felt strange to refer to him this way, as a **man**—as a **sort** of man, a type to be classified. It felt distancing, he was an **a** and not **the**, not **the** friend in question, not **her** friend, **her** Bryn. She felt compelled to be specific now, to be vulnerable in her specificity. Anything general could be dismissed as further politeness, the politeness of expressing regret. To be polite in that manner she needn't have come—a card, a note with flowers would have sufficed. Discomfort had brought her here, she realized, not a desire to comfort and be comforted. Perhaps the discomfort was penance, although it wasn't merely that. It was a last offering of real closeness, of her real self.

She paused.

"I've been thinking, I wish I would have cleaned the bathroom." Bryn frowned reflexively, dismissively, but Ella continued: "I wish I would have brought over dinner.

I wish I would have hugged you the day your mother died." Ella sighed shakily. She shivered a little, just as she had back when she and Alix used to argue late into the night, it was as if the intensity of feeling ate up all her heat, left her teeth chattering and her shoulders stiff with chill. They seldom fought now. They were happier together now than they'd known they could be, back in those more difficult times when they'd first moved in together. Ella looked around the terribly familiar room. She looked into Bryn's familiar gaze and echoed her words from earlier, "I did an adequate job as an employee, but I didn't do well by you as a"—here she paused again—"a friend. I was afraid. I thought I was afraid of overstepping my role, of making you uncomfortable, because you're so private." This statement again felt impersonal, distancing. What did she really know about his character, his tendencies? In her head she'd sometimes felt she was an expert on him; at other times she'd found him unknowable. He maybe didn't apply that word to himself, **private**, especially where she was concerned. She had seen those swollen wrists, that scabbing skin. She had seen the deflated bed pillows. She had seen his face and his hands, and he'd seen hers. Perhaps calling him private could even be considered a kind of mockery, he'd had so little privacy, like suggesting he'd stood naked with his hands uselessly clasped to cover his groin, curled in wretchedly to hide himself when so much was already on display.

"Maybe those fears were fair," she said, "but I've realized that, for me, they were only excuses. I was afraid of the weight of your burden." That sounded stilted, possibly stilted and resentful—so formal! And also perhaps the word he'd least wanted to identify with through all that had occurred. He would have feared being burdensome, he must have, she knew. But how else to express what she felt?

"I wanted a safe remove, I didn't want to feel too much of your sadness," she said. "I don't know how to say this. I did feel your sadness, but—" She winced a little at the presumption that she could have known, even to a degree, his suffering. "I mean, I was in this house, and, well, something was happening to you. But something was happening to me, too, this was my life for a time, too, a part of my life, and I had to keep it from flooding me. I thought I had to. But maybe I was wrong. I think I owed you more. I could have carried more of what you carried. I know I could have."

"You didn't owe me any of that," Bryn said, the patience in his tone and even the gentleness a barrier like age.

Ella started to cry. "I'm sorry," she choked out. "This is embarrassing." Bryn shifted his gaze away uncomfortably, although there was concern in his brow and in the way he held himself, neither open nor newly closed.

"I don't want to be the sort of person who does what's safe. I want to do what's **kind**." Ella had wanted to say "what's **loving**," but she lost her nerve and, anyway, this suddenly seemed dangerously near to being about her, about salvaging her character, and she hadn't meant it like that. She didn't mean she wished she were more kind. She meant she wanted to be ferocious in her kindness. She wasn't asking Bryn to believe that she was a better person than she appeared; she was asking him to see the spirit of her aspirational self and even her aspirational world.

"Ella," he said, "you are very kind. I don't know why you're being so hard on yourself."

Ella calmed her voice and said, "I didn't come here for reassurance, Bryn." She so rarely said his name aloud that it felt almost an endearment, and she was aware of how girlish her voice sounded saying it. She didn't want to seem coy, and this wasn't working, whatever she was doing. How to change it? Frustrated, she said, "It's like I skimped on the cut of meat to make sure I had enough for the flowers. I just wish I'd cleaned the bathroom, that's all! I wish I had. I wish I'd **had** to clean the bathroom, that something inside me had demanded it. Something inside me did demand it but I didn't listen. What was I saving my hands for? To hold yours? You didn't want them held." She choked this through tears and thought wildly for a moment he would reach for her hand to disprove it, but he didn't. Their moment had passed, if it had ever really occurred. He was almost broken with fatigue, but he was no longer drowning. He was in a sad but reasonable place, a clear vantage point from which to take in their substantial age difference and all of the unwelcome complications it entailed.

Ella smeared at her tears with her hands and laughed ruefully. "Anyway," she said, and he touched her shoulder briefly, silently, and then he said, with his familiar shielding cheer, "It's clean now!" She laughed obligingly to help shift the mood. They rose in near unison and walked to the door together and he handed her an envelope of money, a thank-you bonus. She had intended to say, as she left, what she had truly come to say: "I wish I could have loved you better," but with the money in her hand it felt impossible. "See you around," she said, and she walked down the steps into the street.

ACKNOWLEDGMENTS

With many thanks to my family: Iva, Lynn, Robin, Hannah, Solveig, and Evelyn, and to my mentors, Elizabeth Tallent and Lan Samantha Chang. I'd also like to thank my agent, Chris Parris-Lamb, and my editors, Robin Desser and Hannah Westland. Much gratitude to my early readers and supporters: Andy Axel; Brian Ball; Ryan Bradley; John Carroll; Ann Cash; Karen Chapek; Tameka Cage Conley; Barb Davis; Dave Drummond; Ben, Sophie, and Sam Elwood; Steven Fletcher; Benjamin Flowers; Malcolm Gilmour; Mallory Hellman; Kelene Koval; Mark Labowskie; Gabriella Levine; Martin Markowitz;

Acknowledgments

Ben Miyamoto; Navid Mohseni; Siyanda Mohutsiwa; Michelle Morby; Ottessa Moshfegh; Daniel Nazer; Okwiri Oduor; Kate Petersen; Ed Porter; Carissa Potter; Peter Rachleff; Josephine Rowe; Kari Rudd; Earl Schwartz; Lewis Simpler; Susie Steinbach; Michael Swiderski; Jackie Thomas-Kennedy; and Tobias Wolff. This book wouldn't exist without the generous support of Stanford University's Wallace Stegner Fellowship and the University of Iowa Writers' Workshop, as well as the Michener-Copernicus Society, James Patterson, and the University of Iowa College of Liberal Arts and Sciences. Finally, thank you to the clients and families I've worked with over the years— I have learned so much from you.

A NOTE ABOUT THE AUTHOR

Lila Savage is originally from Minneapolis.
Prior to writing fiction, she spent nearly
a decade working as a caregiver. She is a
recipient of a Wallace Stegner Fellowship
and a graduate of the Iowa Writers'
Workshop, and her work has appeared in
The Threepenny Review. She lives in San
Francisco.